True Irish Ghost Stories

Haunted Houses, Banshees, Poltergeists, and Other Supernatural Phenomena

Compiled by St. John D. Seymour
and Harry L. Neligan

DOVER PUBLICATIONS, INC.
Mineola, New York

Bibliographical Note

This Dover edition, first published in 2005, is an unabridged republication of the second edition (enlarged) of the work originally published in 1926 by Hodges, Figgis & Co., Dublin, and Humphrey Milford, London, under the title *True Irish Ghost Stories*. (The first edition was published in 1914.)

Library of Congress Cataloging-in-Publication Data

True Irish ghost stories : haunted houses, banshees, poltergeists, and other supernatural phenomena / compiled by St. John D. Seymour and Harry L. Neligan.
    p. cm.
Originally published: Dublin : Hodges, Figgis & Co., 1926.
ISBN-13: 978-0-486-44051-4 (pbk.)
ISBN-10: 0-486-44051-6 (pbk.)
  1. Ghost stories. 2. Ghosts—Ireland. I. Seymour, St. John D. (St. John Drelincourt) II. Neligan, Harry.

BF1472.T78 2005
133.1'09415—dc22

2005041432

Manufactured in the United States by LSC Communications
44051607   2017
www.doverpublications.com

To
three lively poltergeists
W__, J__, G__.
this book is dedicated
by the compilers.

Contents

CHAPTER I

Ĝaunted Ĝouses in or Near Dublin

Of all species of ghostly phenomena, that commonly known as "haunted houses" appeals most to the ordinary person. There is something very eerie in being shut up within the four walls of a house with a ghost. The poor human being is placed at such a disadvantage. If we know that a gateway, or road, or field has the reputation of being haunted, we can in nearly every case make a detour, and so avoid the unpleasant locality. But the presence of a ghost in a house creates a very different state of affairs. It appears and disappears at its own sweet will, with a total disregard for our feelings: it seems to be as much part and parcel of the domicile as the staircase or the hall door, and, consequently, nothing short of leaving the house or of pulling it down (both of these solutions are not always practicable) will free us absolutely from the unwelcome presence.

There is also something so natural, and at the same time so unnatural, in seeing a door open when we know that no human hand rests on the knob, or in hearing the sound of footsteps, light or heavy, and feeling that it cannot be attributed to the feet of mortal man or woman. Or perhaps a form appears in a room, standing, sitting, or walking—in fact, situated in its three dimensions apparently as an ordinary being of flesh and blood, until it proves its unearthly nature by vanishing before our astonished eyes. Or perhaps we are asleep in bed. The room is shrouded in darkness, and our recumbent attitude, together with the weight of bed-clothes, hampers our

1

movements and probably makes us more cowardly. A man will meet pain or danger boldly if he be standing upright—occupying that erect position which is his as Lord of Creation; but his courage does not well so high if he be supine. We are awakened suddenly by the feel that some superhuman Presence is in the room. We are transfixed with terror, we cannot find either the bell-rope or the matches, while we *dare* not leap out of bed and make a rush for the door lest we should encounter we know not what. In an agony of fear, we feel it moving towards us; it approaches closer, and yet closer, to the bed, and—for what may or may not then happen we must refer our readers to the pages of this book.

But the skeptical reader will say: "This is all very well, but—there are *no* haunted houses. All these alleged strange happenings are due to a vivid imagination, or else to rats and mice." (The question of deliberate and conscious fraud may be rejected in almost every instance.) This simple solution has been put forward so often that it should infallibly have solved the problem long ago. But will such a reader explain how it is that the noise made by rats and mice can resemble slow, heavy footsteps, or else take the form of a human being seen by several persons; or how our imagination can cause doors to open and shut, or else create a conglomeration of noises which, physically, would be beyond the power of ordinary individuals to reproduce? Whatever may be the ultimate explanation, we feel that there is a great deal in the words quoted by Professor Barrett: "In spite of all reasonable skepticism, it is difficult to avoid accepting, at least provisionally, the conclusion that there are, in a certain sense, haunted houses, *i.e.* that there are houses in which similar quasi-human apparitions have occurred at different times to different inhabitants, under circumstances which exclude the hypothesis of suggestion or expectation."

We must now turn to the subject of this chapter. Mrs. G. Kelly, a lady well known in musical circles in Dublin, sends as her own

2

personal experience the following tale of a most quiet haunting, in which the spectral charwoman (!) does not seem to have entirely laid aside all her mundane habits.

"My first encounter with a ghost occurred about twenty years ago. On that occasion I was standing in the kitchen of my house in —————— Square, when a woman, whom I was afterwards to see many times, walked down the stairs into the room. Having heard the footsteps outside, I was not in the least perturbed, but turned to look who it was, and found myself looking at a tall, stout, elderly woman, wearing a bonnet and old-fashioned mantle. She had grey hair, and a benign and amiable expression. We stood gazing at each other while one could count twenty. At first I was not at all frightened, but gradually as I stood looking at her an uncomfortable feeling, increasing to terror, came over me. This caused me to retreat farther and farther back, until I had my back against the wall, and then the apparition slowly faded.

"This feeling of terror, due perhaps to the unexpectedness of her appearance, always overcame me on the subsequent occasions on which I saw her. These occasions numbered twelve or fifteen, and I have seen her in every room in the house, and at every hour of the day, during a period of about ten years. The last time she appeared was ten years ago. My husband and I had just returned from a concert at which he had been singing, and we sat for some time over supper, talking about the events of the evening. When at last I rose to leave the room, and opened the dining-room door, I found my old lady standing on the mat outside with her head bent towards the door in the attitude of listening. I called out loudly, and my husband rushed to my side. That was the last time I have seen her.

"One peculiarity of this spectral visitant was a strong objection to disorder or untidyness of any kind, or even to an alteration in the general routine of the house. For instance, she showed her disapproval of any stranger coming to sleep by turning the chairs face downwards on the floor in the room they were to occupy. I well remember one of our guests, having gone to his room one evening for something he had forgotten, remarking on coming downstairs again, 'Well, you people have an extraordinary manner of arranging your furniture! I have nearly broken my bones over one of the bedroom chairs which was turned down on the floors.' As my husband and I had restored that chair twice already to its proper position during the day, we were not much surprised at his remarks, although we did not enlighten him. The whole family have been disturbed by a peculiar knocking which occurred in various rooms in the house, frequently on the door or wall, but sometimes on the furniture, quite close to where we had been sitting. This was evidently loud enough to be heard in the next house, for our next-door neighbour once asked my husband why he selected such curious hours for hanging his pictures. Another strange and fairly frequent occurrence was the following. I had got a set of skunk furs which I fancied had an unpleasant odour, as this fur sometimes has; and at night I used to take it from my wardrobe and lay it on a chair in the drawing-room, which was next my bedroom. The first time that I did this, on going to the drawing-room I found, to my surprise, my muff in one corner and my stole in another. Not for a moment suspecting a supernatural agent, I asked my servant about it, and she assured me that she had not been in the room that morning. Whereupon I determined to test the matter, which I did by putting in the furs late at night, and taking care that I was the first to enter the room in the morning. I invariably found that they had been disturbed."

The following strange and pathetic incident occurred in a well-known Square in the north side of the city. In or about a hundred years ago a young officer was ordered to Dublin, and took a house there for himself and his family. He sent on his wife and two children, intending to join them in the course of a few days.

4

When the latter and the nurse arrived, they found only the old charwoman in the house, and she left shortly after their arrival. Finding that something was needed, the nurse went out to purchase it. On her return she asked the mother were the children all right, as she had seen two ghostly forms flit past her on the door-step! The mother answered that she believed they were, but on going up to the nursery they found both the children with their throats cut. The murderer was never brought to justice, and no motive was ever discovered for the crime. The unfortunate mother went mad, and it is said that an eerie feeling still clings to the house, while two little heads are sometimes seen at the window of the room where the deed was committed.

A most weird experience fell to the lot of Major Macgregor, and was contributed by him to *Real Ghost Stories*, the celebrated Christmas number of the *Review of Reviews*. He says: "In the end of 1871 I went over to Ireland to visit a relative living in a Square in the north side of Dublin. In January 1872 the husband of my relative fell ill. I sat up with him for several nights, and at last, as he seemed better, I went to bed, and directed the footman to call me if anything went wrong. I soon fell asleep, but some time after was awakened by a push on the left shoulder. I started up, and said, 'Is there anything wrong?' I got no answer, but immediately received another push. I got annoyed, and said 'Can you not speak, man! and tell me if there is anything wrong.' Still no answer, and I had a feeling I was going to get another push when I suddenly turned round and caught a human hand, warm, plump, and soft. I said, 'Who are you?' but I got no answer. I then tried to pull the person towards me, but could not do so. I then said, 'I *will* know who you are!' and having the hand tight in my right hand, with my left I felt the wrist and arm, enclosed, as it seemed to me, in a tight-fitting sleeve of some winter material with a linen cuff, but when I got to the elbow all trace of an arm ceased. I was so astounded that I let the hand go, and just then the clock struck two. Including the mistress of the house, there were five females in the establishment, and I can assert that the hand belonged to none of them. When I reported the adventure, the servants exclaimed, 'Oh, it must have been the master's old Aunt Betty, who lived for many years in the upper part of that house, and had died over fifty years before at a great age.' I afterwards heard that the room in which I felt the hand had been considered haunted, and very curious noises and peculiar incidents occurred, such as the bed-clothes torn off, &c. One lady got a slap in the face from some invisible hand, and when she lit her candle she saw as if something opaque fell or jumped off the bed. A general officer, a brother of the lady, slept there two nights, but preferred going to a hotel to remaining the third night. He never would say what he heard or saw, but always said the room was uncanny. I slept for months in the room afterwards, and was never in the least disturbed."

A truly terrifying sight was witnessed by a clergyman in a school-house a good many years ago. This cleric was curate of a Dublin parish, but resided with his parents some distance out of town in the direction of Malahide. It not infrequently happened that he had to hold meetings in the evenings, and on such occasions, as his home was so far away, and as the modern convenience of tramcars was not then known, he used to sleep in the schoolroom, a large bare room, where the meetings were held. He had made a sleeping-apartment for himself by placing a pole across one end of the room, on which he had rigged up two curtains which, when drawn together, met in the middle. One night he had been holding some meeting, and when everybody had left he locked up the empty schoolhouse, and went to bed. It was a bright moonlight night, and every object could be seen perfectly clearly. Scarcely had he got into bed when he became conscious of some invisible presence. Then he saw the curtains agitated at one end, as if hands were grasping them on the outside. In an agony of terror he watched these hands groping along outside the curtains till they reached the middle. The curtains were then drawn a little apart, and a Face peered in—an awful, evil Face, with an expression of wickedness and hate upon it which no words could describe. It looked at him for a few moments, then drew back again, and the curtains closed. The clergyman had sufficient courage left to leap out of bed and make a thorough examination of the room, but, as he expected, he found no one. He dressed himself as quickly as possible, walked home, and never again slept a night in that schoolroom.

The following tale, sent by Mr. E. B. de Lacy, contains a most extraordinary and unsatisfactory element of mystery. He says: "When I was a boy I lived in the suburbs, and used to come in every morning to school in the city. My way lay through a certain street in which stood a very dismal semi-detached house, which, I might say, was closed up regularly about every six months. I would see new tenants coming into it, and then in a few months it would be 'To let' again. This went on for eight or nine years, and I often wondered what was the reason. On inquiring one day from a friend, I was told that it had the reputation of being haunted.

"A few years later I entered business in a certain office, and one day it fell to my lot to have to call on the lady who at that particular period was the tenant of the haunted house. When we had transacted our business she informed me that she was about to leave. Knowing the reputation of the house, and being desirous of investigating a ghost-story, I asked her if she would give me the history of the house as far as she knew it, which she very kindly did as follows:

"About forty years ago the house was left by will to a gentleman named ———. He lived in it for a short time, when he suddenly went mad, and had to be put in an asylum. Upon this his agents let the house to a lady. Apparently nothing unusual happened for some time, but a few months later, as she went down one morning to a room behind the kitchen, she found the cook hanging by a rope attached to a hook in the ceiling. After the inquest the lady gave up the house.

"It was then closed up for some time, but was again advertised 'To let,' and a caretaker, a woman, was put into it. One night about one o'clock, a constable going his rounds heard some one calling for help from the house, and found the caretaker on the sill of one of the windows holding on as best she could. He told her to go in and open the hall door and let him in, but she refused to enter the room again. He forced open the door and succeeded in dragging the woman back into the room, only to find she had gone mad.

"Again the house was shut up, and again it was let, this time to a lady, on a five-years' lease. However, after a few months' residence, she locked it up, and went away. On her friends asking her why she did so, she replied that she would rather pay the whole five years' rent than live in it herself, or allow anyone else to do so, but would give no other reason.

"'I believe I was the next person to take this house,' said the lady who narrated the story to me (*i.e.* Mr. de Lacy). 'I took it about eighteen months ago on a three years' lease in the hopes of making money by taking in boarders, but I am now giving it up because none of them will stay more than a week or two. They do not give any definite reason as to why they are leaving; they are careful to state that it is not because they have any fault to find with me or my domestic arrangements, but they merely say *they do not like the rooms!* The rooms themselves, as you can see, are good, spacious, and well lighted. I have had all classes of professional men; one of the last was a barrister, and he said that he had no fault to find except that *he did not like the rooms!* I myself do not believe in ghosts, and I have never seen anything strange here or elsewhere; and if I had known the house had the reputation of being haunted, I would never have rented it.'

Marsh's library, that quaint, old-world repository of ponderous tomes, is reputed to be haunted by the ghost of its founder, Primate Narcissus Marsh. He is said to frequent the inner gallery, which contains what was formerly his own private library: he moves in and out among the cases, taking down books from the shelves, and occasionally throwing them down on the reader's desk as if in anger. However, he always leaves things in perfect order. The late Mr. ———, who for some years lived in the librarian's rooms underneath, was a firm believer in this ghost, and said he frequently heard noises which could only be accounted for by the presence of a nocturnal visitor; the present tenant is more sceptical. The story goes that Marsh's niece eloped from the Palace, and was married in a tavern to the curate of Chapelizod. She is reported to have written a note consenting to the elopement, and to have then placed it in one of her uncle's books to which her lover had access, and where he found it. As a punishment for his lack of vigilance, the Archbishop is said to be condemned to hunt for the note until he find it—hence the ghost.

The ghost of a deceased Canon was seen in one of the Dublin cathedrals by several independent witnesses, one of whom, a lady, gives her own experience as follows: "Canon ——— was a personal friend of mine, and we had many times discussed ghosts and spiritualism, in which he was a profound believer, having had many supernatural experiences himself. It was during the Sunday morning service in the cathedral that I saw my friend, who had been dead for two years, sitting inside the communion-rails. I was so much astonished at the flesh-and-blood appearance of the figure that I took off my glasses and wiped them with my handkerchief, at the same time looking away from him down the church. On looking back again he was still there, and continued to sit there for about ten or twelve minutes, after which he faded away. I remarked a change in his personal appearance, which was, that his beard was longer and whiter than when I had known him—in fact, such a change as would have occurred *in life* in the space of two years. Having told my husband of the occurrence on our way home, he remembered having heard some talk of an appearance of this clergyman in the cathedral since his death. He hurried back to the afternoon service, and asked the robestress if anybody had seen Canon ————'s ghost. She informed him that *she* had, and that he had also been seen by one of the sextons in the cathedral. I mention this because in describing his personal appearance she had remarked the same change as I had with regard to the beard."

Some years ago a family had very uncanny experiences in a house in Rathgar, and subsequently in another in Rathmines. These were communicated by one of the young ladies to Mrs. M. A. Wilkins, who published them in the *Journal* of the American S.P.R.,[1] from which they are here taken. The Rathgar house had a basement passage leading to a door into the yard, and along this passage her mother and the children used to hear dragging, limping steps, and the latch of the door rattling, but no one could ever be found when search was made. The house-bells were old and all in a row, and on one occasion they all rang, apparently of their own accord. The lady narrator used to sleep in the back drawing room, and always when the light was put out she heard strange noises, as if some one was going round the room rubbing paper along the wall, while she often had the feeling that a person was standing beside her bed. A cousin, who was a nurse, once slept with her, and also noticed these strange noises. On one occasion this room was given up to a very matter-of-fact young man to sleep in, and next morning he said that the room was very strange, with queer noises in it.

Her mother also had an extraordinary experience in the same house. One evening she had just put the baby to bed, when she

[1] For September 1913.

heard a voice calling "mother." She left the bedroom, and called to her daughter, who was in a lower room, "What do you want?" But the girl replied that she had *not* called her; and then, in her turn, asked her mother if *she* had been in the front room, for she had just heard a noise as if some one was trying to fasten the inside bars of the shutters across. But her mother had been upstairs, and no one was in the front room. The experiences in the Rathmines house were of a similar auditory nature, *i.e.* the young ladies heard their names called, though it was found that no one in the house had done so.

Occasionally it happens that ghosts inspire a law-suit. In the seventeenth century they were to be found actively urging the adoption of legal proceedings, but in the nineteenth and twentieth centuries they play a more passive part. A case about a haunted house took place in Dublin in the year 1885, in which the ghost may be said to have won. A Mr. Waldron, a solicitor's clerk, sued his next-door neighbour, one Mr. Kiernan, a mate in the merchant service, to recover £500 for damages done to his house.

Kiernan altogether denied the charges, but asserted that Waldron's house was notoriously haunted. Witnesses proved that every night, from August 1884 to January 1885, stones were thrown at the windows and doors, and extraordinary and inexplicable occurrences constantly took place.

Mrs. Waldron, wife of the plaintiff, swore that one night she saw one of the panes of glass of a certain window cut through with a diamond, and a white hand inserted through the hole. She at once caught up a bill-hook and aimed a blow at the hand, cutting off one of the fingers. This finger could not be found, nor were any traces of blood seen.

A servant of hers was sorely persecuted by noises and the sound of footsteps. Mr. Waldron, with the aid of detectives and policemen, endeavoured to find out the cause, but with no success. The witnesses in the case were closely cross-examined, but without shaking their testimony. The facts appeared to be proved, so the jury found for Kiernan, the defendant. At least twenty persons had testified on oath to the fact that the house had been known to have been haunted.

Before leaving the city and its immediate surroundings, we must relate the story of an extraordinary ghost, somewhat lacking in good manners, yet not without a certain distorted sense of humour. Absolutely incredible though the tale may seem, yet it comes on very good authority. It was related to our informant, Mr. D., by a Mrs. C., whose daughter he had employed as governess. Mrs. C., who is described as "a woman of respectable position and good education," heard it in her turn from her father and mother. In the story the relationship of the different persons seems a little involved, but it would appear that the initial A belongs to the surname both of Mrs. C.'s father and grandfather.

This ghost was commonly called "Corney" by the family, and he answered to this though it was not his proper name. He disclosed this latter to Mr. C.'s mother, who forgot it. Corney made his presence manifest to the A— family shortly after they had gone to reside in ———— Street in the following manner. Mr. A— had sprained his knee badly, and had to use a crutch, which at night was left at the head of his bed. One night his wife heard some one walking on the lobby, thump, thump, thump, as if imitating Mr. A—. She struck a match to see if the crutch had been removed from the head of the bed, but it was still there.

From that on Corney commenced to talk, and he spoke every day from his usual habitat, the coal-cellar off the kitchen. His voice sounded as if it came out of an empty barrel.

He was very troublesome, and continually played practical jokes on the servants, who, as might be expected, were in terror of their lives of him; so much so that Mrs. A— could hardly induce them to stay with her. They used to sleep in a press-bed in the kitchen, and in order to get away from Corney, they asked for a room at the top of the house, which was given to them. Accordingly the press-bed was moved up there. The first night they went to retire to bed after the change, the doors of the press were flung open, and Corney's voice said, "Ha! ha! you devils, I am here before you! I am not confined to any particular part of this house."

Corney was continually tampering with the doors, and straining locks and keys. He only manifested himself in material form to two persons; to ———, who died with the fright, and to Mr. A— (Mrs. C.'s father) when he was about seven years old. The latter described him to his mother as a naked man, with a curl on his forehead, and a skin like a clothes-horse (!).

One day a servant was preparing fish for dinner. She laid it on the kitchen table while she went elsewhere for something she wanted. When she returned the fish had disappeared. She there-upon began to cry, fearing she would be accused of making away with it. The next thing she heard was the voice of Corney from the coal-cellar saying, "There, you blubbering fool, is your fish for you!" and, suiting the action to the word, the fish was thrown out on the kitchen floor.

Relatives from the country used to bring presents of vegetables, and these were often hung up by Corney like Christmas decorations round the kitchen. There was one particular press in the kitchen he would not allow anything into. He would throw it out again. A crock with meat in pickle was put into it, and a fish placed on the cover of the crock. He threw the fish out.

Silver teaspoons were missing, and no account of them could be got until Mrs. A— asked Corney to confess if he had done anything with them. He said, "They are under the ticking in the servants' bed." He had, so he said, a daughter in ——— Street, and sometimes announced that he was going to see her, and would not be here to-night.

On one occasion he announced that he was going to have "company" that evening, and if they wanted any water out of the soft-

13

water tank, to take it before going to bed, as he and his friends would be using it. Subsequently that night five or six distinct voices were heard, and next morning the water in the tank was as black as ink, and not alone that, but the bread and butter in the pantry were streaked with the marks of sooty fingers.

A clergyman in the locality, having heard of the doings of Corney, called to investigate the matter. He was advised by Mrs. A— to keep quiet, and not to reveal his identity, as being the best chance of hearing Corney speak. He waited a long time, and as the capricious Corney remained silent, he left at length. The servants asked, "Corney, why did you not speak?" and he replied, "I could not speak while that good man was in the house." The servants sometimes used to ask him where he was. He would reply, "The Great God would not permit me to tell you. I was a bad man, and I died the death." He named the room in the house in which he died.

Corney constantly joined in any conversation carried on by the people of the house. One could never tell when a voice from the coal-cellar would erupt into the dialogue. He had his likes and dislikes: he appeared to dislike anyone that was not afraid of him, and would not talk to them. Mrs. C.'s mother, however, used to get good of him by coaxing. An uncle, having failed to get him to speak one night, took the kitchen poker, and hammered at the door of the coal-cellar, saying, "I'll make you speak"; but Corney wouldn't. Next morning the poker was found broken in two. This uncle used to wear spectacles, and Corney used to call him derisively, "Four-eyes." An uncle named Richard came to sleep one night, and complained in the morning that the clothes were pulled off him. Corney told the servants in great glee, "I slept on Master Richard's feet all night."

Finally Mr. A— made several attempts to dispose of his lease, but with no success, for when intending purchasers were being shown over the house and arrived at Corney's domain, the spirit would begin to speak and the would-be purchaser would fly.

14

They asked him if they changed house would he trouble them. He replied, "No! but if they throw down this house, I will trouble the stones."

At last Mrs. A— appealed to him to keep quiet, and not to injure people who had never injured him. He promised that he would do so, and then said, "Mrs. A—, you will be all right now, for I see a lady in black coming up the street to this house, and she will buy it." Within half an hour a widow called and purchased the house. Possibly Corney is still there, for our informant looked up the Directory as he was writing, and found the house marked "Vacant."

Near Blanchardstown, Co. Dublin, is a house, occupied at present, or up to very recently, by a private family; it was formerly a monastery, and there are said to be secret passages in it. Once a servant ironing in the kitchen saw the figure of a nun approach the kitchen window and look in. Our informant was also told by a friend (now dead), who had it from the lady of the house, that once night falls, no doors can be kept closed. If anyone shuts them, almost immediately they are flung open again with the greatest violence and apparent anger. If left open there is no trouble or noise, but light footsteps are heard, and there is a vague feeling of people passing to and fro. The persons inhabiting the house are matter-of-fact, unimaginative people, who speak of this as if it were an everyday affair. "So long as we leave the doors unclosed they don't harm us: why should we be afraid of them?" Mrs. —— said. Truly a most philosophical attitude to adopt!

A haunted house in Kingstown, Co. Dublin, was investigated by Professor W. Barrett and Professor Henry Sidgwick. The story is singularly well attested (as one might expect from its being inserted in the pages of the *Proceedings S.P.R.*[1]), as the apparition

[1] July 1884, p. 141.

was seen on three distinct occasions, and by three separate persons who were all personally known to the above gentlemen. The house in which the following occurrences took place is described as being a very old one, with unusually thick walls. The lady saw her strange visitant in her bedroom. She says: "Disliking cross-lights, I had got into the habit of having the blind of the back window drawn and the shutters closed at night, and of leaving the blind raised and the shutters opened towards the front, liking to see the trees and sky when I awakened. Opening my eyes now one morning, I saw right before me (this occurred in July 1873) the figure of a woman, stooping down and apparently looking at me. Her head and shoulders were wrapped in a common woollen shawl; her arms were folded, and they were also wrapped, as if for warmth, in the shawl. I looked at her in my horror, and dared not cry out lest I might move the awful thing to speech or action. Behind her head I saw the window and the growing dawn, the looking-glass upon the toilet-table, and the furniture in that part of the room. After what may have been only seconds—of the duration of this vision I cannot judge—she raised herself and went backwards towards the window, stood at the toilet-table, and gradually vanished. I mean she grew by degrees transparent, and that through the shawl and the grey dress she wore I saw the white muslin of the tablecover again, and at last saw that only in the place where she had stood." The lady lay motionless with terror until the servant came to call her. The only other occupants of the house at the time were her brother and the servant, to neither of whom did she make any mention of the circumstance, fearing that the former would laugh at her, and the latter give notice.

Exactly a fortnight later, when sitting at breakfast, she noticed that her brother seemed out of sorts, and did not eat. On asking him if anything were the matter, he answered, "I have had a horrid nightmare—indeed it was no nightmare: I saw it early this morning, just as distinctly as I see you." "What?" she asked. "A villainous-looking hag," he replied, "with her head and arms wrapped in a cloak, stooping over me, and looking like this—" He got up, folded his arms, and put himself in the exact posture of the vision. Whereupon she informed him of what she herself had seen a fortnight previously.

About four years later, in the same month, the lady's married sister and two children were alone in the house. The eldest child, a boy of about four or five years, asked for a drink, and his mother went to fetch it, desiring him to remain in the dining-room until her return. Coming back she met the boy pale and trembling, and on asking him why he left the room, he replied, "Who is that woman—who is that woman?" "Where?" she asked. "That old woman who went upstairs," he replied. So agitated was he, that she took him by the hand and went upstairs to search, but no one was to be found, though he still maintained that a woman went upstairs. A friend of the family subsequently told them that a woman had been killed in the house many years previously, and that it was reported to be haunted.

CHAPTER II

Haunted Houses in Conn's Half

From a very early period a division of Ireland into two "halves" existed. This was traditionally believed to have been made by Conn the Hundred-fighter and Mogh Nuadat, in A.D. 166. The north was in consequence known as Conn's Half, the south as Mogh's Half, the line of division being a series of gravel hills extending from Dublin to Galway. This division we have followed, except that we have included the whole of the counties of West Meath and Galway in the northern portion. We had hoped originally to have had *four* chapters on Haunted Houses, one for each of the four provinces, but, for lack of material from Connaught, we have been forced to adopt the plan on which Chapters I-III are arranged.

Mrs. Acheson, of Co. Roscommon, sends the following: "Emo House, Co. Westmeath, a very old mansion since pulled down, was purchased by my grandfather for his son, my father. The latter had only been living in it for a few days when knocking commenced at the hall door. Naturally he thought it was someone playing tricks, or endeavouring to frighten him away. One night he had the lobby window open directly over the door. The knocking commenced, and he looked out: it was a very bright night, and as there was no porch he could see the door distinctly; the knocking continued, but he did not see the knocker move. Another night he sat up expecting his brother, but as the latter

19

did not come he went to bed. Finally the knocking became so loud and insistent that he felt sure his brother must have arrived. He went downstairs and opened the door, but no one was there. Still convinced that his brother was there and had gone round to the yard to put up his horse, he went out; but scarcely had he gone twenty yards from the door when the knocking recommenced behind his back. On turning round he could see no one.

"After this the knocking got very bad, so much so that he could not rest. All this time he did not mention the strange occurrence to anyone. One morning he went up through the fields between four and five o'clock. To his surprise he found the herd out feeding the cattle. My father asked him why he was up so early. He replied that he could not sleep. 'Why?' asked my father. 'You know why yourself, sir—the knocking.' He then found that this man had heard it all the time, though he slept at the end of a long house. My father was advised to take no notice of it, for it would go as it came, though at this time it was continuous and very loud; and so it did. The country people said it was the late resident who could not rest.

"We had another curious and most eerie experience in this house. A former rector was staying the night with us, and as the evening wore on we commenced to tell ghost-stories. He related some remarkable experiences, and as we were talking the drawing-room door suddenly opened as wide as possible, and then slowly closed again. It was a calm night, and at any rate it was a heavy double door which never flies open however strong the wind may be blowing. Everyone in the house was in bed, as it was after 12 o'clock, except the three persons who witnessed this, viz. myself, my daughter, and the rector. The effect on the latter was most marked. He was a big, strong, jovial man and a good athlete, but when he saw the door open he quivered like an aspen leaf."

A strange story of a haunting, in which nothing was seen, but in which the same noises were heard by different people, is sent by one of the percipients, who does not wish to have her name disclosed. She says: "When staying for a time in a country house in the North of Ireland some years ago I was awakened on several nights by hearing the tramp, tramp, of horses' hoofs. Sometimes it sounded as if they were walking on paving-stones, while at other times I had the impression that they were going round a large space, and as if someone was using a whip on them. I heard neighing, and champing of bits, and so formed the impression that they were carriage horses. I did not mind it much at first, as I thought the stables must be near that part of the house. After hearing these noises several times I began to get curious, so one morning I made a tour of the place. I found that the side of the house I occupied overlooked a neglected garden, which was mostly used for drying clothes. I also discovered that the stables were right at the back of the house, and so it would be impossible for me to hear any noises in that quarter; at any rate there was only one farm horse left, and this was securely fastened up every night. Also there were no cobble-stones round the yard. I mentioned what I had heard to the people of the house, but as they would give me no satisfactory reply I passed it over. I did not hear these noises every night.

"One night I was startled out of my sleep by hearing a dreadful disturbance in the kitchen. It sounded as if the dish-covers were being taken off the wall and dashed violently on the flagged floor. At length I got up and opened the door of my bedroom, and just as I did so an appalling crash resounded through the house. I waited to see if there was any light to be seen, or footstep to be heard, but nobody was stirring. There was only one servant in the house, the other persons being my host, his wife, and a baby, who had all retired early. Next morning I described the noises in the kitchen to the servant, and she said she had often heard them. I then told her about the tramping of horses: she replied that she herself had never heard it, but that other persons who had occupied my room had had experiences similar

21

to mine. I asked her was there any explanation; she said No, except that a story was told of a gentleman who had lived there some years ago, and was very much addicted to racing and gambling, and that he was shot one night in that house. For the remainder of my visit I was removed to another part of the house, and I heard no more noises."

A house in the North of Ireland, near that locality which is eternally famous as having furnished the material for the last trial for witchcraft in the country, is said to be haunted, the reason being that it is built on the site of a disused and very ancient graveyard. It is said that when some repairs were being carried out nine human skulls were unearthed. It would be interesting to ascertain how many houses in Ireland are traditionally said to be built on such unpleasant sites, and if they all bear the reputation of being haunted. The present writer knows of one, in the South, which is so situated (and this is supported, to a certain extent, by documentary evidence from the thirteenth century down) and which in consequence has an uncanny reputation. But concerning the above house it has been found almost impossible to get any information. It is said that strange noises were frequently heard there, which sometimes seemed as if cartloads of stones were being run down one of the gables. On one occasion an inmate of the house lay dying upstairs. A friend went up to see the sick person, and on proceeding to pass through the bedroom door was pressed and jostled as if by some unseen person hurriedly leaving the room. On entering, it was found that the sick person had just passed away.

An account of a most unpleasant haunting is contributed by Mr. W. S. Thompson, who vouches for the substantial accuracy of it, and also furnishes the names of two men, still living, who attended the "station." We give it as it stands, with the comment that some of the details seem to have been grossly exaggerated by local raconteurs. In the year 1869 a ghost made its presence manifest in the house of a Mr. M— in Co. Cavan. In the daytime it resided in the chimney, but at night it left its quarters and subjected the family to considerable annoyance. During the day they could cook nothing, as showers of soot would be sent down the chimney on top of every pot and pan that was placed on the fire. At night the various members of the family would be dragged out of bed by the hair, and pulled around the house. When anyone ventured to light a lamp it would immediately be put out, while chairs and tables would be sent dancing round the room. At last matters reached such a pitch that the family found it impossible to remain any longer in the house. The night before they left Mrs. M— was severely handled, and her boots left facing the door as a gentle hint for her to be off. Before they departed some of the neighbours went to the house, saw the ghost, and even described to Mr. Thompson what they had seen. According to one man it appeared in the shape of a human being with a pig's head with long tusks. Another described it as a horse with an elephant's head, and a headless man seated on its back. Finally a "station" was held at the house by seven priests, at which all the neighbours attended. The station commenced after sunset, and everything in the house had to be uncovered, lest the evil spirit should find any resting-place. A free passage was left out of the door into the street, where many people were kneeling. About five minutes after the station opened a rumbling noise was heard, and a black barrel rolled out with an unearthly din, though to some coming up the street it appeared in the shape of a black horse with a bull's head, and a headless man seated thereon. From this time the ghost gave no further trouble.

The same gentleman also sends an account of a haunted shop in which members of his family had some very unpleasant experiences. "In October 1882 my father, William Thompson, took over the grocery and spirit business from a Dr. S— to whom it had been left by will. My sister was put in charge of the business, and she slept on the premises at night, but she was not there by herself very long until she found things amiss. The third night matters were made so unpleasant for her that she had to get up out of bed more dead than alive, and go across the street to Mrs. M—, the servant at the R.I.C. barrack, with whom she remained until the morning. She stated that as she lay in bed, half awake and half asleep, she saw a man enter the room, who immediately seized her by the throat and well-nigh choked her. She had only sufficient strength left to gasp 'Lord, save me!' when instantly the man vanished. She also said that she heard noises as if every bottle and glass in the shop was smashed to atoms, yet in the morning everything would be found intact. My brother was in charge of the shop one day, as my sister had to go to Belturbet to do some Christmas shopping. He expected her to return to the shop that night, but as she did not do so he was preparing to go to bed about 1 A.M., when suddenly a terrible noise was heard. The light was extinguished, and the tables and chairs commenced to dance about the floor, and some of them struck him on the shins. Upon this he left the house, declaring that he had seen the Devil!" Possibly this ghost had been a rabid teetotaller in the flesh, and continued to have a dislike to the publican's trade after he had become discarnate. At any rate the present occupants, who follow a different avocation, do not appear to be troubled.

Ghosts are no respecters of persons or places, and take up their quarters where they are least expected. One can hardly imagine them entering a R.I.C. barrack, and annoying the stalwart inmates thereof. Yet more than one tale of a haunted police-barrack has been sent to us—nay, in its proper place we shall relate the appearance of a deceased member of the "Force," uniform and all! The following personal experiences are contributed by an ex-R.I.C. constable, who requested that all names should be suppressed. "The barrack of which I am about to speak has now disappeared, owing to the construction of a new railway line. It was a three-storey house, with large airy apartments and splendid accommodation. This particular night I was on guard. After the constables had retired to their quarters I took my palliasse downstairs to the day-room, and laid it on two forms alongside two six-foot tables which were placed end to end in the centre of the room.

"As I expected a patrol in at midnight, and as another had to be sent out when it arrived, I didn't promise myself a very restful night, so I threw myself on the bed, intending to read a bit, as there was a large lamp on the table. Scarcely had I commenced to read when I felt as if I was being pushed off the bed. At first I thought I must have fallen asleep, so to make sure, I got up, took a few turns around the room, and then deliberately lay down again and took up my book. Scarcely had I done so, when the same thing happened, and, though I resisted with all my strength, I was finally landed on the floor. My bed was close to the table, and the pushing came from that side, so that if anyone was playing a trick on me they could not do so without being under the table: I looked, but there was no visible presence there. I felt shaky, but changed my couch to another part of the room, and had no further unpleasant experience. Many times after I was 'guard' in the same room, but I always took care not to place my couch in that particular spot.

"One night, long afterwards, we were all asleep in the dormitory, when we were awakened in the small hours of the morning by the guard rushing upstairs, dashing through the room, and jumping into a bed in the farthest corner behind its occupant. There he lay gasping, unable to speak for several minutes, and even then we couldn't get a coherent account of what befel him. It appears he fell asleep, and suddenly awoke to find himself on the floor, and a body rolling over him. Several men volunteered to go downstairs with him, but he absolutely refused to leave the dormitory, and stayed there till morning. Nor would he even remain downstairs at night without having a comrade with him. It ended in his applying for an exchange of stations.

"Another time I returned off duty at midnight, and after my comrade, a married Sergeant, had gone outside to his quarters I went to the kitchen to change my boots. There was a good fire on, and it looked so comfortable that I remained toasting my toes on the hob, and enjoying my pipe. The lock-up was a lean-to one-storey building off the kitchen, and was divided into two cells, one opening into the kitchen, the other into that cell. I was smoking away quietly when I suddenly heard inside the lock-up a dull, heavy thud, just like the noise a drunken man would make by crashing down on all-fours. I wondered who the prisoner could be, as I didn't see anyone that night who seemed a likely candidate for free lodgings. However as I heard no other sound I decided I would tell the guard in order that he might look after him. As I took my candle from the table I happened to glance at the lock-up, and, to my surprise, I saw that the outer door was open. My curiosity being roused, I looked inside, to find the inner door also open. There was nothing in either cell, except the two empty plank-beds, and these were immovable as they were firmly fixed to the walls. I betook myself to my bedroom much quicker than I was in the habit of doing.

"I mentioned that this barrack was demolished owing to the construction of a new railway line. It was the last obstacle removed, and in the meantime workmen came from all points of the compass. One day a powerful navvy was brought into the barrack a total collapse from drink, and absolutely helpless. After his neckwear was loosened he was carried to the lock-up and laid on the plank-bed, the guard being instructed to visit him periodically, lest he should smother. He was scarcely half an hour there—this was in the early evening—when the most unmerciful screaming brought all hands to the lock-up, to find the erstwhile helpless man standing on the plank-bed, and grappling with a, to us, invisible foe. We took him out, and he maintained that a man had tried to choke him, and was still there when we came to his relief. The strange thing was, that he was shivering with fright, and perfectly sober, though in the ordinary course of events he would not be in that condition for at least seven or eight hours. The story spread like wildfire through the town, but the inhabitants were not in the least surprised, and one old man told us that many strange things happened in that house long before it became a police-barrack."

A lady, who requests that her name be suppressed, relates a strange sight seen by her sister in Galway. The latter's husband was stationed in that town about seventeen years ago. One afternoon he was out, and she was lying on a sofa in the drawing-room, when suddenly from behind a screen (where there was no door) came a little old woman, with a small shawl over her head and shoulders, such as the country women used to wear. She had a most diabolical expression on her face. She seized the lady by the hand, and said: "I will drag you down to Hell, where I am!" The lady sprang up in terror and shook her off, when the horrible creature again disappeared behind the screen. The house was an old one, and many stories were rife amongst the people about it, the one most to the point being that the apparition of an old woman, who was supposed to have poisoned someone, used to be seen therein. Needless to say, the lady in question never again sat by herself in the drawing-room.

Two stories are told about haunted houses at Drogheda, the one by A. G. Bradley in *Notes on some Irish Superstitions* (Drogheda, 1894), the other by F. G. Lee in *Sights and Shadows* (p. 42). As both appear to be placed at the same date, *i.e.* 1890, it is quite possible that they refer to one and the same haunting, and we have so treated them accordingly. The reader, if he wishes, can test the matter for himself.

This house, which was reputed to be haunted, was let to a tailor and his wife by the owner at an annual rent of £23. They took possession in due course, but after a very few days they became aware of the presence of a most unpleasant supernatural lodger. One night, as the tailor and his wife were preparing to retire, they were terrified at seeing the foot of some invisible person kick the candlestick off the table, and so quench the candle. Although it was a very dark night, and the shutters were closed, the man and his wife could see everything in the room just as well as if it were the middle of the day. All at once a woman entered the room, dressed in white, carrying something in her hand, which she threw at the tailor's wife, striking her with some violence, and then vanished. While this was taking place on the first floor, a most frightful noise was going on overhead in the room where the children and their nurse were sleeping. The father immediately rushed upstairs, and found to his horror the floor all torn up, the furniture broken, and, worst of all, the children lying senseless and naked on the bed, and having the appearance of having been severely beaten. As he was leaving the room with the children in his arms he suddenly remembered that he had not seen the nurse, so he turned back with the intention of bringing her downstairs, but could find her nowhere. The girl, half-dead with fright, and very much bruised, had fled to her mother's house, where she died in a few days in agony.

Because of these occurrences they were legally advised to refuse to pay any rent. The landlady, however, declining to release them from their bargain, at once claimed a quarter's rent; and when this remained for some time unpaid, sued them for it before Judge Kisby. A Drogheda solicitor appeared for the tenants, who, having given evidence of the facts concerning the ghost in question, asked leave to support their sworn testimony by that of several other people. This, however, was disallowed by the judge. It was admitted by the landlady that nothing on one side or the other had been said regarding the haunting when the house was let. A judgment was consequently entered for the landlady, although it had been shown indirectly that unquestionably the house had had the reputation of being haunted, and that previous tenants had been much inconvenienced.

This chapter may be concluded with two stories dealing with haunted rectories. The first, and mildest, of these is contributed by the present Dean of St. Patrick's; it is not his own personal experience, but was related to him by a rector in Co. Monaghan, where he used to preach on special occasions. The rector and his daughters told the Dean that they had often seen in that house the apparition of an old woman dressed in a drab cape, while they frequently heard noises. On one evening the rector was in the kitchen together with the cook and the coachman. All three heard noises in the pantry as if vessels were being moved. Presently they saw the old woman in the drab cape come out of the pantry and move up the stairs. The rector attempted to follow her, but the two servants held him tightly by the arms, and besought him not to do so. But hearing the children, who were in bed, screaming, he broke from the grip of the servants and rushed upstairs. The children said that they had been frightened by seeing a strange old woman coming into the room, but she was now gone. The house had a single roof, and there was no way to or from the nursery except by the stairs. The rector stated that he took to praying that the old woman might have rest, and that it was now many years since she had been seen. A very old parishioner told him that when she was young she remembered having seen an old woman answering to the rector's description, who had lived in the house, which at that time was not a rectory.

The second of these, which is decidedly more complex and mystifying, refers to a rectory in Co. Donegal. It is sent as the personal experience of one of the percipients, who does not wish to have his name disclosed. He says: "My wife, children, and myself will have lived here four years next January (1914). From the first night that we came into the house most extraordinary noises have been heard. Sometimes they were inside the house, and seemed as if the furniture was being disturbed, and the fire-

29

irons knocked about, or at other times as if a dog was running up and down stairs. Sometimes they were external, and resembled tin buckets being dashed about the yard, or as if a herd of cattle was galloping up the drive before the windows. These things would go on for six months, and then everything would be quiet for three months or so, when the noises would commence again. My dogs—a fox-terrier, a boar-hound, and a spaniel—would make a terrible din, and would bark at something in the hall we could not see, backing away from it all the time.

"The only thing that was ever *seen* was as follows: One night my daughter went down to the kitchen about ten o'clock for some hot water. She saw a tall man, with one arm, carrying a lamp, who walked out of the pantry into the kitchen, and then through the kitchen wall. Another daughter saw the same man walk down one evening from the loft, and go into the harness-room. She told me, and I went out immediately, but could see nobody. Shortly after that my wife, who is very brave, heard a knock at the hall door in the dusk. Naturally thinking it was some friend, she opened the door, and there saw standing outside the selfsame man. He simply looked at her, and walked through the wall into the house. She got such a shock that she could not speak for several hours, and was ill for some days. That is eighteen months ago, and he has not been seen since, and it is six months since we heard any noises." Our correspondent's letter was written on 25th November 1913. "An old man nearly ninety died last year. He lived all his life within four hundred yards of this house, and used to tell me that seventy years ago the parsons came with bell, book, and candle to drive the ghosts out of the house." Evidently they were unsuccessful. In English ghost-stories it is the parson who performs the exorcism successfully, while in Ireland such work is generally performed by the priest. Indeed a tale was sent to us in which a ghost quite ignored the parson's efforts, but succumbed to the priest.

CHAPTER III

ђaunted ђouses in Mogh's ђalf

THE NORTHERN HALF of Ireland has not proved as prolific in stories of haunted houses as the southern portion: the possible explanation of this is, not that the men of the north are less prone to hold, or talk about, such beliefs, but that, as regards the south half, we have had the good fortune to happen upon some diligent collectors of these and kindred tales, whose eagerness in collecting is only equalled by their kindness in imparting information to the compilers of this book.

On a large farm near Portarlington there once lived a Mrs. ——, a strong minded, capable woman, who managed all her affairs for herself, giving her orders, and taking none from anybody. In due time she died, and the property passed to the next-of-kin. As soon, however, as the funeral was over, the house was nightly disturbed by strange noises: people downstairs would hear rushings about in the upper rooms, banging of doors, and the sound of heavy footsteps. The cups and saucers used to fall off the dresser, and all the pots and pans would rattle.

This went on for some time, till the people could stand it no longer, so they left the house and put in a herd and his family. The latter was driven away after he had been in the house a few weeks. This happened to several people, until at length a man named Mr. B— took the house. The noises went on as before until some one suggested getting the priest in. Accordingly the priest

31

came, and held a service in the late Mrs. ——'s bedroom. When this was over, the door of the room was locked. After that the noises were not heard till one evening Mr. B— came home from a fair, fortified, no doubt, with a little "Dutch courage," and declared that even if the devil were in it he would go into the locked room. In spite of all his family could say or do, he burst open the door, and entered the room, but apparently saw nothing. That night pandemonium reigned in the house, the chairs were hurled about, the china was broken, and the most weird and uncanny sounds were heard. Next day the priest was sent for, the room again shut up, and nothing has happened from that day to this.

Another strange story comes from the same town. "When I was on a visit to a friend in Portarlington," writes a lady in the *Journal* of the American S.P.R (September, 1913) "a rather unpleasant incident occurred to me. At about two o'clock in the morning I woke up suddenly, for apparently no reason whatever; however, I quite distinctly heard snoring coming from under or in the bed in which I was lying. It continued for about ten minutes, during which time I was absolutely limp with fright. The door opened, and my friend entered the bedroom, saying, 'I thought you might want me, so I came in.' Needless to say, I hailed the happy inspiration that sent her to me. I then told her what I had heard; she listened to me, and then to comfort (!) me said, 'Oh, never mind; *it is only grandfather!* He died in this room, and a snoring is heard every night at two o'clock, the hour at which he passed away.' Some time previously a German gentleman was staying with this family. They asked him in the morning how he had slept, and he replied that he was disturbed by a snoring in the room, but he supposed it was the cat."

A lady, formerly resident in Queen's Co., but who now lives near Dublin, sends the following clear and concise account of her own personal experiences in a haunted house: "Some years ago, my father, mother, sister, and myself went to live in a nice but rather small house close to the town of —— in Queen's Co. We liked the house, as it was conveniently and pleasantly situated, and we certainly never had a thought of ghosts or haunted houses, nor would my father allow any talk about such things in his presence. But we were not long settled there when we were disturbed by the opening of the parlour door every night regularly at the hour of eleven o'clock. My father and mother used to retire to their room about ten o'clock, while my sister and I used to sit up reading. We always declared that we would retire before the door opened, but we generally got so interested in our books that we would forget until we would hear the handle of the door turn, and see the door flung open. We tried in every way to account for this, but we could find no explanation, and there was no possibility of any human agent being at work.

"Some time after, light was thrown on the subject. We had visitors staying with us, and in order to make room for them, my sister was asked to sleep in the parlour. She consented without a thought of ghosts, and went to sleep quite happily; but during the night she was awakened by some one opening the door, walking across the room, and disturbing the fireirons. She, supposing it to be the servant, called her by name, but got no answer: then the person seemed to come away from the fireplace, and walk out of the room. There was a fire in the grate, but though she heard the footsteps, she could see no one.

"The next thing was, that I was coming downstairs, and as I glanced towards the hall door I saw standing by it a man in a grey suit. I went to my father and told him. He asked in surprise who let him in, as the servant was out, and he himself had already locked, bolted, and chained the door an hour previously. None of us had let him in, and when my father went out to the hall the man had disappeared, and the door was as he had left it.

"Some little time after, I had a visit from a lady who knew the place well, and in the course of conversation she said:

"'This is the house poor Mr. —— used to live in.'

"'Who is Mr.——?' I asked.

"'Did you never hear of him?' she replied. 'He was a minister who used to live in this house quite alone, and was murdered in this very parlour. His landlord used to visit him sometimes, and one night he was seen coming in about eleven o'clock, and was seen again leaving about five o'clock in the morning. When Mr. —— did not come out as usual, the door was forced open, and he was found lying dead in this room by the fender, with his head battered in with the poker.'

"We left the house soon after," adds our informant.

The following weird incidents occurred, apparently in the Co. Kilkenny, to a Miss K. B., during two visits paid by her to Ireland in 1880 and 1881. The house in which she experienced the following was really an old barrack, long disused, very old-fashioned, and surrounded with a high wall: it was said that it had been built during the time of Cromwell as a stronghold for his men. The only inhabitants of this were Captain C— (a retired officer in charge of the place), Mrs. C—, three daughters, and two servants. They occupied the central part of the building, the mess-room being their drawing-room. Miss K. B.'s bedroom was very lofty, and adjoined two others which were occupied by the three daughters, E., G., and L.

"The first recollection I have of anything strange," writes Miss B., "was that each night I was awakened about three o'clock by a tremendous noise, apparently in the next suite of rooms, which was empty, and it sounded as if some huge iron boxes and other heavy things were being thrown about with great force. This continued for about half an hour, when in the room underneath (the kitchen) I heard the fire being violently poked and raked for several minutes, and this was immediately followed

34

by a most terrible and distressing cough of a man, very loud and violent. It seemed as if the exertion had brought on a paroxysm which he could not stop. In large houses in Co. Kilkenny the fires are not lighted every day, owing to the slow-burning property of the coal, and it is only necessary to rake it up every night about eleven o'clock, and in the morning it is still bright and clear. Consequently I wondered why it was necessary for Captain C— to get up in the middle of the night to stir it so violently."

A few days later Miss B. said to E. C.: "I hear such strange noises every night—are there any people in the adjoining part of the building?" She turned very pale, and looking earnestly at Miss B., said, "Oh K., I am so sorry you heard. I hoped no one but myself had heard it. I could have given worlds to have spoken to you last night, but dared not move or speak." K. B. laughed at her for being so superstitious, but E. declared that the place was haunted, and told her of a number of weird things that had been seen and heard.

In the following year, 1881, Miss K. B. paid another visit to the barrack. This time there were two other visitors there—a colonel and his wife. They occupied Miss B.'s former room, while to her was allotted a huge bedroom on the top of the house, with a long corridor leading to it; opposite to this was another large room, which was occupied by the girls.

Her strange experiences commenced again. "One morning, about four o'clock, I was awakened by a very noisy martial footstep ascending the stairs, and then marching quickly up and down the corridor outside my room. Then suddenly the most violent coughing took place that I ever heard, which continued for some time, while the quick, heavy step continued its march. At last the footsteps faded away in the distance, and I then recalled to mind the same coughing after exertion last year." In the morning, at breakfast, she asked both Captain C— and the colonel had they been walking about, but both denied, and also said they had no cough. The family looked very uncomfortable, and afterwards E. came up with tears in her eyes, and said, "Oh K., please don't say anything more about that dreadful coughing; we all hear it often, especially when anything terrible is about to happen."

Some nights later the C—s gave a dance. When the guests had departed, Miss B. went to her bedroom. "The moon was shining so beautifully that I was able to read my Bible by its light, and had left the Bible open on the window-sill, which was a very high one, and on which I sat to read, having had to climb the washstand to reach it. I went to bed, and fell asleep, but was not long so when I was suddenly awakened by the strange feeling that some one was in the room. I opened my eyes, and turned around, and saw on the window-sill in the moonlight a long, very thin, very dark figure bending over the Bible, and apparently earnestly scanning the page. As if my movement disturbed the figure, it suddenly darted up, jumped off the window-ledge on to the washstand, then to the ground, and flitted quietly across the room to the table where my jewellery was." That was the last she saw of it. She thought it was some one trying to steal her jewellery, so waited till morning, but nothing was missing. In the morning she described to one of the daughters, G., what she had seen, and the latter told her that something always happened when that appeared. Miss K. B. adds that nothing did happen. Later on she was told that a colonel had cut his throat in that very room.

Another military station, Charles Fort, near Kinsale, has long had the reputation of being haunted. An account of this was sent to the *Wide World Magazine* (Jan. 1908), by Major H. L. Ruck Keene, D.S.O.; he states that he took it from a manuscript written by a Captain Marvell Hull about the year 1880. Further information on the subject of the haunting is to be found in Dr. Craig's *Real Pictures of Clerical Life in Ireland.*

Charles Fort was erected in 1667 by the Duke of Ormonde. It is said to be haunted by a ghost known as the "White Lady," and the traditional account of the reason for this haunting is briefly as follows: Shortly after the erection of the fort, a Colonel Warrender, a severe disciplinarian, was appointed its governor. He had a daughter, who bore the quaint Christian name of "Wilful"; she became engaged to a Sir Trevor Ashurst, and subsequently married him. On the evening of their wedding-day the bride and bridegroom were walking on the battlements, when she espied some flowers growing on the rocks beneath. She expressed a wish for them, and a sentry posted close by volunteered to climb down for them, provided Sir Trevor took his place during his absence. He assented, and took the soldier's coat and musket while he went in search of a rope. Having obtained one, he commenced his descent; but the task proving longer than he expected, Sir Trevor fell asleep. Meantime the governor visited the sentries, as was his custom, and in the course of his rounds came to where Sir Trevor was asleep. He challenged him, and on receiving no answer perceived that he was asleep, whereupon he drew a pistol and shot him through the heart. The body was brought in, and it was only then the governor realised what had happened. The bride, who appears to have gone indoors before the tragedy occurred, then learned the fate that befell her husband, and in her distraction, rushed from the house and flung herself over the battlements. In despair at the double tragedy, her father shot himself during the night.

The above is from Dr. Craig's book already alluded to. In the *Wide World Magazine* the legend differs slightly in details. According to this the governor's name was Browne, and it was his own son, not his son-in-law, that he shot; while the incident is said to have occurred about a hundred and fifty years ago.

The "White Lady" is the ghost of the young bride. Let us see what accounts there are of her appearance. A good many years ago Fort-Major Black, who had served in the Peninsular War, gave his own personal experience to Dr. Craig. He stated that he had gone to the hall door one summer evening, and saw a lady entering the door and going up the stairs. At first he thought she was an officer's wife, but as he looked, he observed she was dressed in white, and in a very old-fashioned style. Impelled by curiosity, he hastened upstairs after her, and followed her closely into one of the rooms, but on entering it he could not find the slightest trace of anyone there. On another occasion he stated that two sergeants were packing some cast stores. One of them had his little daughter with him, and the child suddenly exclaimed, "Who is that white lady who is bending over the banisters, and looking down at us?" The two men looked up, but could see nothing, but the child insisted that she had seen a lady in white looking down and smiling at her.

On another occasion a staff officer, a married man, was residing in the "Governor's House." One night as the nurse lay awake —she and the children were in a room which opened into what was known as the White Lady's apartment—she suddenly saw a lady clothed in white glide to the bedside of the youngest child, and after a little place her hand upon its wrist. At this the child started in its sleep, and cried out, "Oh! take that cold hand from my wrist!" the next moment the lady disappeared.

One night, about the year 1880, Captain Marvell Hull and Lieutenant Hartland were going to the rooms occupied by the former officer. As they reached a small landing they saw distinctly in front of them a woman in a white dress. As they stood there in awestruck silence she turned and looked towards them, showing a face beautiful enough, but colourless as a corpse, and then passed on through a locked door.

But it appears that this presence did not always manifest itself in as harmless a manner. Some years ago Surgeon L— was quartered at the fort. One day he had been out snipe-shooting, and as he entered the fort the mess-bugle rang out. He hastened to his rooms to dress, but as he failed to put in an appearance at mess, one of the officers went in search of him, and found him lying senseless on the floor. When he recovered consciousness he related his experience. He said he had stooped down for the key of his door, which he had placed for safety under the mat; when in this position he felt himself violently dragged across the hall, and flung down a flight of steps. With this agrees somewhat the experience of a Captain Jarves, as related by him to Captain Marvell Hull. Attracted by a strange rattling noise in his bedroom, he endeavoured to open the door of it, but found it seemingly locked. Suspecting a hoax, he called out, whereupon a gust of wind passed him, and some unseen power flung him down the stairs, and laid him senseless at the bottom.

Near a seaside town in the south of Ireland a group of small cottages was built by an old lady, in one of which she lived, while she let the others to her relatives. In process of time all the occupants died, the cottages fell into ruin, and were all pulled down (except the one in which the old lady had lived), the materials being used by a farmer to build a large house which he hoped to let to summer visitors. It was shortly afterwards taken for three years by a gentleman for his family. It should be noted that the house had very bare surroundings; there were no trees near, or outhouses where people could be concealed. Soon after the family came to the house they began to hear raps all over it, on doors, windows, and walls; these raps varied in nature, sometimes being like a sledgehammer, loud and dying away, and sometimes quick and sharp, two or three or five in succession; and all heard them. One morning about 4 A.M., the mother heard very loud knocking on the bedroom door; thinking it was the servant wanting to go to early mass, she said, "Come in," but the knocking continued till the father was awakened by it; he got up, searched the house, but could find no one. The servant's door was slightly open, and he saw that she was sound asleep. That morning a telegram came announcing the death of a beloved uncle just about the hour of the knocking. Some time previous to this the mother was in the kitchen, when a loud explosion took place beside her, startling her very much, but no cause for it could be found, nor were any traces left. This coincided with the death of an aunt, wife to the uncle who died later.

One night the mother went to her bedroom. The blind was drawn, and the shutters closed, when suddenly a great crash came, as if a branch was thrown at the window, and there was a sound of broken glass. She opened the shutters with the expectation of finding the window smashed, but there was not even a crack in it. She entered the room next day at one o'clock, and the same crash took place, being heard by all in the house: she went in at 10 A.M. on another day, and the same thing happened, after which she refused to enter that room again.

Another night, after 11 P.M., the servant was washing up in the kitchen, when heavy footsteps were heard by the father and mother going upstairs, and across a lobby to the servant's room; the father searched the house, but could find no one. After that footsteps used to be heard regularly at that hour, though no one could ever be seen walking about.

The two elder sisters slept together, and used to see flames shooting up all over the floor, though there was no smell or heat; this used to be seen two or three nights at a time, chiefly in the one room. The first time the girls saw this one of them got up and went to her father in alarm, naturally thinking the room underneath must be on fire.

The two boys were moved to the haunted room [which one?], where they slept in one large bed with its head near the chimney-piece. The elder boy, aged about thirteen, put his watch on the mantelpiece, awoke about 2 A.M., and wishing to ascertain the time, put his hand up for his watch; he then felt a deathly cold hand laid on his. For the rest of that night the two boys were terrified by noises, apparently caused by two people rushing about the room fighting and knocking against the bed. About 6 A.M. they went to their father, almost in hysterics from terror, and refused to sleep there again. The eldest sister, not being nervous, was then given that room; she was, however, so disturbed by these noises that she begged her father to let her leave it, but having no other room to give her, he persuaded her to stay there, and at length she got accustomed to the noise, and could sleep in spite of it. Finally the family left the house before their time was up.

Mr. T. J. Westropp, to whom we are indebted for so much material, sends a tale which used to be related by a relative of his, the Rev. Thomas Westropp, concerning experiences in a house not very far from the city of Limerick. When the latter was appointed to a certain parish he had some difficulty in finding a suitable house, but finally fixed on one which had been untenanted for many years, but had nevertheless been kept aired and in good repair, as a caretaker who lived close by used to come and look after it every day. The first night that the family settled there, as the clergyman was going upstairs he heard a footstep and the rustle of a dress, and as he stood aside a lady passed him, entered a door facing the stairs, and closed it after her. It was only then he realised that her dress was very old-fashioned, and that he had not been able to enter that particular room. Next day he got assistance from a carpenter, who, with another man, forced open the door. A mat of cobwebs fell as they did so, and the floor and windows were thick with dust. The men went across the room, and as the clergyman followed them he saw a small white bird flying round the ceiling; at his exclamation the men looked back and also saw it. It swooped, flew out of the door, and they did not see it again. After that the family were alarmed by hearing noises under the floor of that room every night. At length the clergyman had the boards taken up, and the skeleton of a child was found underneath. So old did the remains appear that the coroner did not deem it necessary to hold an inquest on them, so the rector buried them in the church-yard. Strange noises continued, as if some one were trying

41

to force up the boards from underneath. Also a heavy ball was heard rolling down the stairs and striking against the study door. One night the two girls woke up screaming, and on the nurse running up to them, the elder said she had seen a great black dog with fiery eyes resting its paws on her bed. Her father ordered the servants to sit constantly with them in the evenings, but, notwithstanding the presence of two women in the nursery, the same thing occurred. The younger daughter was so scared that she never quite recovered. The family left the house immediately.

The same correspondent says: "An old ruined house in the hills of east Co. Clare enjoyed the reputation of being 'desperately haunted' from, at any rate, 1865 down to its dismantling. I will merely give the experiences of my own relations, as told by them to me. My mother told how one night she and my father heard creaking and grating, as if a door were being forced open. The sound came from a passage in which was a door nailed up and clamped with iron bands. A heavy footstep came down the passage, and stopped at the bedroom door for a moment; no sound was heard, and then the 'thing' came through the room to the foot of the bed. It moved round the bed, they not daring to stir. The horrible unseen visitant stopped, and they *felt* it watching them. At last it moved away, they heard it going up the passage, the door crashed, and all was silence. Lighting a candle, my father examined the room, and found the door locked; he then went along the passage, but not a sound was to be heard anywhere.

"Strange noises like footsteps, sobbing, whispering, grim laughter, and shrieks were often heard about the house. On one occasion my eldest sister and a girl cousin drove over to see the family and stayed the night. They and my two younger sisters were all crowded into a huge, old-fashioned bed, and carefully drew and tucked in the curtains all round. My eldest sister awoke feeling a cold wind blowing on her face, and putting out her hand found the curtains drawn back and, as they subsequently discovered, wedged between the bed and the wall. She reached for the match-box, and was about to light the candle when a horrible mocking laugh rang out close to the bed, which awakened the other girls. Being always a plucky woman, though then badly scared, she struck a match, and searched the room, but nothing was to be seen. The closed room was said to have been deserted after a murder, and its floor was supposed to be stained with blood which no human power could wash out."

Another house in Co. Clare, nearer the estuary of the Shannon, which was formerly the residence of the D— family, but is now pulled down, had some extraordinary tales told about it in which facts (if we may use the word) were well supplemented by legend. To commence with the former. A lady writes: "My father and old Mr. D— were first cousins. Richard D— asked my father would he come and sit up with him one night, in order to see what might be seen. Both were particularly sober men. The annoyances in the house were becoming unbearable. Mrs. D—'s work-box used to be thrown down, the table-cloth would be whisked off the table, the fender and fireirons would be hurled about the room, and other similar things would happen. Mr. D— and my father went up to one of the bedrooms, where a big fire was made up. They searched every part of the room carefully, but nothing uncanny was to be seen or found. They then placed two candles and a brace of pistols on a small table between them, and waited. Nothing happened for some time, till all of a sudden a large black dog walked out from under the bed. Both men fired, and the dog disappeared. That is all! The family had to leave the house."

Now to the blending of fact with fiction, of which we have already spoken: the intelligent reader can decide in his own mind which is which. It was said that black magic had been practised in this house at one time, and that in consequence terrible and weird occurrences were quite the order of the day there. When being cooked, the hens used to scream and the mutton used to bleat in the pot. Black dogs were seen frequently. The beds used to be lifted up, and the occupants thereof used to be beaten black and blue, by invisible hands. One particularly ghoulish tale was told. It was said that a monk (!) was in love with one of the daughters of the house, who was an exceedingly fat girl. She died unmarried, and was buried in the family vault. Some time later the vault was again opened for an interment, and those who entered it found that Miss D—'s coffin had been disturbed, and the lid loosened. They then saw that all the fat around her heart had been scooped away.

Apropos of ineradicable blood on a floor, which is a not infrequent item in stories of haunted houses, it is said that a manifestation of this nature forms the haunting in a farmhouse in Co. Limerick. According to our informants, a light must be kept burning in this house all night; if by any chance it is forgotten, or becomes quenched, in the morning the floor is covered with blood. The story is evidently much older than the house, but no traditional explanation is given.

Two stories of haunted schools have been sent to us, both on very good authority; these establishments lie within the geographical limits of this chapter, but for obvious reasons, we cannot indicate their locality more precisely, though the names of both are known to us. The first of these was told to our correspondent by the boy Brown, who was in the room, but did *not* see the ghost.

When Brown was about fifteen he was sent to ———— School. His brother told him not to be frightened at anything he might see or hear, as the boys were sure to play tricks on all newcomers. He was put to sleep in a room with another new arrival, a boy named Smith, from England. In the middle of the night Brown was roused from his sleep by Smith crying out in great alarm, and asking who was in the room. Brown, who was very angry at being waked up, told him not to be a fool—that there was no one there. The second night Smith roused him again, this time in greater alarm than the first night. He said he saw a man in cap and gown come into the room with a lamp, and then pass right through the wall. Smith got out of his bed, and fell on his knees beside Brown, beseeching him not to go to sleep. At first Brown thought it was all done to frighten him, but he then saw that Smith was in a state of abject terror. Next morning they spoke of the occurrence, and the report reached the ears of the Head Master, who sent for the two boys. Smith refused to spend another night in the room. Brown said he had seen or heard nothing, and was quite willing to sleep there if another fellow would sleep with him, but he would not care to remain there alone. The Head Master then asked for volunteers from the class of elder boys, but not one of them would sleep in the room. It had always been looked upon as "haunted," but the Master thought that by putting in new boys who had not heard the story they would sleep there all right.

Some years after, Brown revisited the place, and found that another attempt had been made to occupy the room. A new Head Master who did not know its history, thought it a pity to have the room idle, and put a teacher, also new to the school, in possession. When this teacher came down the first morning, he asked who had come into his room during the night. He stated that a man in cap and gown, having books under his arm and a lamp in his hand, came in, sat down at a table, and began to read. He knew that he was not one of the masters, and did not recognise him as one of the boys. The room had to be abandoned. The tradition is that many years ago a master was murdered in that room by one of the students. The few boys who ever had the courage to persist in sleeping in the room said if they stayed more than two or three nights that the furniture was moved, and they heard violent noises.

The second story was sent to us by the percipient herself, and is therefore a first-hand experience. Considering that she was only a schoolgirl at the time, it must be admitted that she made a most plucky attempt to run the ghost to earth.

"A good many years ago, when I first went to school, I did not believe in ghosts, but I then had an experience which caused me to alter my opinion. I was ordered with two other girls to sleep in a small top room at the back of the house which over-looked a garden which contained ancient apple-trees.

"Suddenly in the dead of night I was awakened out of my sleep by the sound of heavy footsteps, as of a man wearing big boots unlaced, pacing ceaselessly up and down a long corridor which I knew was plainly visible from the landing outside my door, as there was a large window at the farther end of it, and there was sufficient moonlight to enable one to see its full length. After listening for about twenty minutes, my curiosity was aroused, so I got up and stood on the landing. The footsteps still continued, but I could see nothing, although the sounds actually reached the foot of the flight of stairs which led from the corridor to the landing on which I was standing. Suddenly the footfall ceased, pausing at my end of the corridor, and I then considered it was high time for me to retire, which I accordingly did, carefully closing the door behind me.

"To my horror the footsteps ascended the stairs, and the bedroom door was violently dashed back against a washing-stand, beside which was a bed; the contents of the ewer were spilled over the occupant, and the steps advanced a few paces into the room in my direction. A cold perspiration broke out all over me; I cannot describe the sensation. It was not actual fear—it was more than that—I felt I had come into contact with the Unknown.

"What was about to happen? All I could do was to speak; I cried out, 'Who are you? What do you want?' Suddenly the footsteps ceased; I felt relieved, and lay awake till morning, but no further sound reached my ears. How or when my ghostly visitant disappeared I never knew; suffice it to say, my story was no nightmare, but an actual fact, of which there was found sufficient proof in the morning; the floor was still saturated with water, the door, which we always carefully closed at night, was wide open, and last, but not least, the occupant of the wet bed had heard all that had happened, but feared to speak, and lay awake till morning.

"Naturally, we related our weird experience to our schoolmates, and it was only then I learned from one of the elder girls that this ghost had manifested itself for many years in a similar fashion to the inhabitants of that room. It was supposed to be the spirit of a man who, long years before, had occupied this apartment (the house was then a private residence), and had commited suicide by hanging himself from an old apple tree opposite the window. Needless to say, the story was hushed up, and we were sharply spoken to, and warned not to mention the occurrence again.

"Some years afterwards a friend, who happened at the time to be a boarder at this very school, came to spend a week-end with me. She related an exactly similar incident which occurred a few nights previous to her visit. My experience was quite unknown to her."

The following account of strange happenings at his glebe-house has been sent by the rector of a parish in the diocese of Cashel: "Shortly after my wife and I came to live here, some ten years ago, the servants complained of hearing strange noises in the top storey of the Rectory where they sleep. One girl ran away the day after she arrived, declaring that the house was haunted, and that nothing would induce her to sleep another night in it. So often had my wife to change servants on this account that at last I had to speak to the parish priest, as I suspected that the idea of 'ghosts' might have been suggested to the maids by neighbours who might have some interest in getting rid of them. I understand that my friend the parish priest spoke very forcibly from the altar on the subject of spirits, saying that the only spirits he believed ever did any harm to anyone were—, mentioning a well-known brand of the wine of the country. Whether this priestly admonition was the cause or not, for some time we heard no more tales of ghostly manifestations.

"After a while, however, my wife and I began to hear a noise which, while in no sense alarming, has proved to be both remarkable and inexplicable. If we happen to be sitting in the dining-room after dinner, sometimes we hear what sounds like the noise of a heavy coach rumbling up to the hall door. We have both heard this noise hundreds of times between eight P.M. and midnight. Sometimes we hear it several times the same night, and then perhaps we won't hear it again for several months. We hear it best on calm nights, and as we are nearly a quarter of a mile from the high road, it is difficult to account for, especially as the noise appears to be quite close to us—I mean not farther away than the hall-door. I may mention that an Englishman was staying with us a few years ago. As we were sitting in the dining-room one night after dinner he said, 'A carriage has just driven up to the door'; but we knew it was only the 'phantom coach,' for we also heard it. Only once do I remember hearing it while sitting in the drawing-room. So much for the 'sound' of the 'phantom coach,' but now I must tell you what I *saw* with my own eyes as clearly as I now see the paper on which I am writing. Some years ago in the middle of the summer, on a scorching hot day, I was out cutting some hay opposite the hall door just by the tennis court. It was between twelve and one o'clock. I remember the time distinctly, as my man had gone to his dinner shortly before. The spot on which I was commanded a view of the avenue from the entrance gate for about four hundred yards. I happened to look up from my occupation—for scything is no easy work—and I saw what I took to be a somewhat high dog-cart, in which two people were seated, turning in at the avenue gate. As I had my coat and waistcoat off, and was not in a state to receive visitors, I got behind a newly-made hay-cock and watched the vehicle until it came to a bend in the avenue where there is a clump of trees which obscured it from my view. As it did not, however, reappear, I concluded that the occupants had either stopped for some reason or had taken by mistake a cart-way leading to the back gate into the garden. Hastily putting on my coat, I went down to the bend in the avenue, but to my surprise there was nothing to be seen.

"Returning to the Rectory, I met my housekeeper, who has been with me for nearly twenty years, and I told her what I had seen. She then told me that about a month before, while I was away from home, my man had one day gone with the trap to the station. She saw, just as I did, a trap coming up the avenue until it was lost to sight owing to the intervention of the clump of trees. As it did not come on, she went down to the bend, but there was no trap to be seen. When the man came in some half-hour after, my housekeeper asked him if he had come half-way up the avenue and turned back, but he said he had only that minute come straight from the station. My housekeeper said she did not like to tell me about it before, as she thought I 'would have laughed at her.' Whether the 'spectral gig' which I saw and the 'phantom coach' which my wife and I have often heard are one and the same I know not, but I do know that what I saw in the full blaze of the summer sun was not inspired by a dose of the spirits referred to by my friend the parish priest.

"Some time during the winter of 1912, I was in the motor-house one dark evening at about 6 P.M. I was working at the engine, and as the car was 'nose in' first, I was, of course, at the farthest point from the door. I had sent my man down to the village with a message. He was gone about ten minutes when I heard heavy footsteps enter the yard and come over to the motor-house. I 'felt' that there was some one in the house quite close to me, and I said, 'Hullo, ——, what brought you back so soon,' as I knew he could not have been to the village and back. As I got no reply, I took up my electric lamp and went to the back of the motor to

49

see who was there, but there was no one to be seen, and although I searched the yard with my lamp, I could discover no one. About a week later I heard the footsteps again under almost identical conditions, but I searched with the same futile result.

"Before I stop, I must tell you about a curious 'presentiment' which happened with regard to a man I got from the Queen's County. He arrived on a Saturday evening, and on the following Monday morning I put him to sweep the avenue. He was at his work when I went out in the motor car at about 10:30 A.M. Shortly after I left he left his wheel-barrow and tools on the avenue (just at the point where I saw the 'spectral gig' disappear) and, coming up to the Rectory, he told my housekeeper in a great state of agitation that he was quite sure that his brother, with whom he had always lived, was dead. He said he must return home at once. My housekeeper advised him to wait until I returned, but he changed his clothes and packed his box, saying he must catch the next train. Just before I returned home at 12 o'clock, a telegram came saying his brother had died suddenly that morning, and that he was to return at once. On my return I found him almost in a state of collapse. He left by the next train, and I never heard of him again."

K— Castle is a handsome blending of ancient castle and modern dwelling-house, picturesquely situated among trees, while the steep glen mentioned below runs close beside it. It has the reputation of being haunted, but, as usual, it is difficult to get information. One gentleman, to whom we wrote, stated that he never saw or heard anything worse than a bat. On the other hand, a lady who resided there a good many years ago, gives the following account of her extraordinary experiences therein:

DEAR MR. SEYMOUR,

I enclose some account of our experiences in K— Castle. It would be better not to mention names, as the people occupying it have told me they are afraid of their servants hearing anything, and consequently giving notice. They themselves hear voices often, but, like me, they do not mind. When first we went there we heard people talking, but on looking everywhere we could find no one. Then on some nights we heard fighting in the glen beside the house. We could hear voices raised in anger, and the clash of steel: no person would venture there after dusk.

One night I was sitting talking with my governess, I got up, said good-night, and opened the door, which was on the top of the back staircase. As I did so, *I heard* some one (a woman) come slowly upstairs, walk past us to a window at the end of the landing, and then with a shriek fall heavily. As she passed it was bitterly cold, and I drew back into the room, but did not say anything, as it might frighten the governess. She asked me what was the matter, as I looked so white. Without answering, I pushed her into her room, and then searched the house, but with no results.

Another night I was sleeping with my little girl. I awoke, and saw a girl with long, fair hair standing at the fireplace, one hand at her side, the other on the chimney-piece. Thinking at first it was my little girl, I felt on the pillow to see if she were gone, but she was fast asleep. There was no fire or light of any kind in the room.

Some time afterwards a friend was sleeping there, and she told me that she was pushed out of bed the whole night. Two gentlemen to whom I had mentioned this came over, thinking they would find out the cause. In the morning when they came down they asked for the carriage to take them to the next train, but would not tell what they had heard or seen. Another person who came to visit her sister, who was looking after the house before we went in, slept in this room, and in the morning said she must go back that day. She also would give no information.

On walking down the corridor, I have heard a door open, a footstep cross before me, and go into another room, *both* doors being closed at the time. An old cook I had told me that when she went into the hall in the morning, a gentleman would come down the front stairs, take a plumed hat off the stand, and vanish *through* the hall door. This she saw nearly every morning. She also said that a girl often came into her bedroom, and put her hand on her (the cook's) face; and when she would push her away she would hear a girl's voice say, "Oh don't!" three times. I have often heard voices in the drawing-room, which decidedly sounded as if an old gentleman and a girl were talking. Noises like furniture being moved were frequently heard at night, and strangers staying with us have often asked why the servants turned out the rooms underneath them at such an unusual hour. The front-door bell sometimes rang, and I have gone down, but found no one.—Yours very sincerely,

F. T.

"Kilman" Castle, in the heart of Ireland—the name is obviously a pseudonym—has been described as perhaps the worst haunted mansion in the British Isles. That it deserves this doubtful recommendation, we cannot say; but at all events the ordinary reader will be prepared to admit that it contains sufficient "ghosts" to satisfy the most greedy ghost-hunter. A couple of months ago the present writer paid a visit to this castle, and was shown all over it one morning by the mistress of the house, who, under the *nom de plume* of "Andrew Merry" has published novels dealing with Irish life, and has also contributed articles on the ghostly phenomena of her house to the *Occult Review* (Dec. 1908 and Jan. 1909).

The place itself is a grim, grey, bare building. The central portion, in which is the entrance-hall, is a square castle of the usual type; it is built on a rock, and a slight batter from base to summit gives an added appearance of strength and solidity. On either side of the castle are more modern wings, one of which terminates in what is known as the "Priest's House."

Now to the ghosts. The top storey of the central tower is a large, well-lighted apartment, called the "Chapel," having evidently served that purpose in times past. At one end is what is said to be an *oubliette*, now almost filled up. Occasionally in the evenings, people walking along the roads or in the fields see the windows of this chapel lighted up for a few seconds as if many lamps were suddenly brought into it. This is certainly *not* due to servants; from our experience we can testify that it is the last place on earth that a domestic would enter after dark. It is also said that a treasure is buried somewhere in or around the castle. The legend runs that an ancestor was about to be taken to Dublin on a charge of rebellion, and, fearing he would never return, made the best of the time left to him by burying somewhere a crock full of gold and jewels. Contrary to expectation, he *did* return; but his long confinement had turned his brain, and he could never remember the spot where he had deposited his treasure years before. Some time ago a lady, a Miss B., who was decidedly psychic, was invited to Kilman Castle in the hope that she would be able to locate the whereabouts of this treasure. In this respect she failed, unfortunately, but gave, nevertheless, a curious example of her power. As she walked through the hall with her hostess, she suddenly laid her hand upon the bare stone wall, and remarked, "There is something uncanny here, but I don't know what it is." In that very spot, some time previously, two skeletons had been discovered walled up.

The sequel to this is curious. Some time after, Miss B. was either trying automatic writing, or else was at a séance (we forget which), when a message came to her from the Unseen, stating that the treasure at Kilman Castle was concealed in the chapel under the tessellated pavement near the altar. But this spirit was either a "lying spirit," or else a most impish one, for there is no trace of an altar, and it is impossible to say, from the style of the room, where it stood; while the tessellated pavement (if it exists) is so covered with the debris of the former roof that it would be almost impossible to have it thoroughly cleared.

There is as well a miscellaneous assortment of ghosts. A monk with tonsure and cowl walks in at one window of the Priest's House, and out at another. There is also a little old man, dressed in the antique garb of a green cut-away coat, knee breeches, and buckled shoes: he is sometimes accompanied by an old lady in similar old-fashioned costume. Another ghost has a penchant for iying on the bed beside its lawful and earthly occupant; nothing is seen, but a great weight is felt, and a consequent deep impression made on the bedclothes.

The lady of the house states that she has a number of letters from friends, in which they relate the supernatural experiences they had while staying at the Castle. In one of these the writer, a gentleman, was awakened one night by an extraordinary feeling of intense cold at his heart. He then saw in front of him a tall female figure, clothed from head to foot in red, and with its right hand raised menacingly in the air: the light which illuminated the figure was from within. He lit a match, and sprang out of bed, but the room was empty. He went back to bed, and saw nothing more that night, except that several times the same cold feeling gripped his heart, though to the touch the flesh was quite warm.

But of all the ghosts in that well-haunted house the most unpleasant is that inexplicable thing that is usually called "It." The lady of the house described to the present writer her personal experience of this phantom. High up round one side of the hall runs a gallery which connects with some of the bedrooms. One evening she was in this gallery leaning on the balustrade, and looking down into the hall. Suddenly she felt two hands laid on her shoulders; she turned round sharply, and saw "It" standing close beside her. She described it as being human in shape, and about four feet high; the eyes were like two black holes in the face, and the whole figure seemed as if it were made of grey cotton-wool, while it was accompanied by a most appalling stench, such as would come from a decaying human body. The lady got a shock from which she did not recover for a long time.

CHAPTER IV

Poltergeists

POLTERGEIST IS THE term assigned to those apparently meaning-less noises and movements of objects of which we from time to time hear accounts. The word is, of course, German, and may be translated "boisterous ghost." A poltergeist is seldom or never seen, but contents itself by moving furniture and other objects about in an extraordinary manner, often contrary to the laws of gravitation; sometimes footsteps are heard, but nothing is visible, while at other times vigorous rappings will be heard either on the walls or floor of a room, and in the manner in which the raps are given a poltergeist has often showed itself as having a close connection with the physical phenomena of spiritualism, for cases have occurred in which a poltergeist has given the exact number of raps mentally asked for by some person present. Another point that is worthy of note is the fact that the hauntings of a poltergeist are generally attached to a certain individual in a certain spot, and thus differ from the operations of an ordinary ghost.

The two following incidents related in this chapter are taken from a paper read by Professor Barrett, F.R.S., before the Society for Psychical Research. In the case of the first anecdote he made every possible inquiry into the facts set forth, short of actually being an eye-witness of the phenomena. In the case of the second he made personal investigation, and himself saw the whole of the incidents related. There is therefore very little room to doubt the genuineness of either story.

In the year 1910, in a certain house in Court Street, Enniscorthy, there lived a labouring man named Redmond. His wife took in boarders to supplement her husband's wages, and at the time to which we refer there were three men boarding with her, who slept in one room above the kitchen. The house consisted of five rooms—two on the ground-floor, of which one was a shop and the other the kitchen. The two other rooms upstairs were occupied by the Redmonds and their servant respectively. The bedroom in which the boarders slept was large, and contained two beds, one at each end of the room, two men sleeping in one of them; John Randall and George Sinnott were the names of two, but the name of the third lodger is not known—he seems to have left the Redmonds very shortly after the disturbances commenced.

It was on July 4, 1910, that John Randall, who is a carpenter by trade, went to live at Enniscorthy, and took rooms with the Redmonds. In a signed statement, now in possession of Professor Barrett, he tells a graphic tale of what occurred each night during the three weeks he lodged in the house, and as a result of the poltergeist's attentions he lost three-quarters of a stone in weight. It was on the night of Thursday, July 7, that the first incident occurred, when the bedclothes were gently pulled off his bed. Of course he naturally thought it was a joke, and shouted to his companions to stop. As no one could explain what was happening, a match was struck, and the bedclothes were found to be at the window, from which the other bed (a large piece of furniture which ordinarily took two people to move) had been rolled just when the clothes had been taken off Randall's bed. Things were put straight and the light blown out, "but," Randall's account goes on to say, "it wasn't long until we heard some hammering in the room—tap-tap-tap-like. This lasted for a few minutes, getting quicker and quicker. When it got very quick, their bed started to move out across the room. . . . We then struck a match and got the lamp. We searched the room thoroughly, and could find nobody. Nobody had come in the door. We called the man of the house (Redmond); he came into the room, saw the bed, and told us to push it back and get into bed (he thought all the time one of us was playing the trick on the other). I said I wouldn't stay in the other bed by myself, so I got in with the others; we put out the light again, and it had only been a couple of minutes out when the bed ran out on the floor with the three of us. Richard struck a match again, and this time we all got up and put on our clothes; we had got a terrible fright and couldn't stick it any longer. We told the man of the house we would sit up in the room till daylight. During the time we were sitting in the room we could hear footsteps leaving the kitchen and coming up the stairs; it would stop on the landing outside the door, and wouldn't come into the room. The footsteps and noises continued through the house until daybreak."

The next night the footsteps and noises were continued, but the unfortunate men did not experience any other annoyance. On the following day the men went home, and it is to be hoped they were able to make up for all the sleep they had lost on the two previous nights. They returned on the Sunday, and from that night till they finally left the house the men were disturbed practically every night. On Monday, 11th July the bed was continually running out from the wall with its three occupants. They kept the lamp alight, and a chair was seen to dance gaily out into the middle of the floor. On the following Thursday we read of the same happenings, with the addition that one of the boarders was lifted out of the bed, though he felt no hand near him. It seems strange that they should have gone through such a bad night exactly a week from the night the poltergeist started its operations. So the account goes on; every night that they slept in the room the hauntings continued, some nights being worse than others. On Friday, 29th July, "the bed turned up on one side and threw us out on the floor, and before we were thrown out, the pillow was taken from under my head three times. When the

57

bed rose up, it fell back without making any noise. This bed was so heavy, it took both the woman and the girl to pull it out from the wall without anybody in it, and there were only three castors on it." The poltergeist must have been an insistent fellow, for when the unfortunate men took refuge in the other bed, they had not been long in it before it began to rise, but could not get out of the recess it was in unless it was taken to pieces.

"It kept very bad," we read, "for the next few nights. So Mr. Murphy, from the *Guardian* office, and another man named Devereux, came and stopped in the room one night."

The experiences of Murphy and Devereux on this night are contained in a further statement, signed by Murphy and corroborated by Devereux. They seem to have gone to work in a business-like manner, as before taking their positions for the night they made a complete investigation of the bedroom and house, so as to eliminate all chance of trickery or fraud. By this time, it should be noted, one of Mrs. Redmond's lodgers had evidently suffered enough from the poltergeist, as only two men are mentioned in Murphy's statement, one sleeping in each bed. The two investigators took up their position against the wall midway between the two beds, so that they had a full view of the room and the occupants of the beds. "The night," says Murphy, "was a clear, starlight night. No blind obstructed the view from outside, and one could see the outlines of the beds and their occupants clearly. At about 11:30 a tapping was heard close at the foot of Randall's bed. My companion remarked that it appeared to be like the noise of a rat eating at timber. Sinnott replied, 'You'll soon see the rat it is.' The tapping went on slowly at first . . . then the speed gradually increased to about a hundred or a hundred and twenty per minute, the noise growing louder. This continued for about five minutes, when it stopped suddenly. Randall then spoke. He said: 'The clothes are slipping off my bed: look at them sliding off. Good God, they are going off me.' Mr. Devereux immediately struck a match, which he had ready in his hand. The bedclothes had partly left the boy's bed, having gone diagonally towards the foot, going out at the left corner, and not alone did they seem to be drawn off the bed, but they appeared to be actually going back under the bed, much in the same position one would expect bedclothes to be if a strong breeze were blowing through the room at the time. But then everything was perfectly calm."

A search was then made for wires or strings, but nothing of the sort could be found. The bedclothes were put back and the light extinguished. For ten minutes silence reigned, only to be broken by more rapping which was followed by shouts from Randall. He was told to hold on to the clothes, which were sliding off again. But this was of little use, for he was heard to cry, "I'm going, I'm going, I'm gone," and when a light was struck he was seen to slide from the bed and all the bedclothes with him. Randall, who, with Sinnott, had shown considerable strength of mind by staying in the house under such trying circumstances, had evidently had enough of ghostly hauntings, for as he lay on the floor, trembling in every limb and bathed in perspiration, he exclaimed: "Oh, isn't this dreadful? I can't stand it; I can't stay here any longer." He was eventually persuaded to get back to bed. Later on more rapping occurred in a different part of the room, but it soon stopped, and the rest of the night passed away in peace.

Randall and Sinnott went to their homes the next day, and Mr. Murphy spent from eleven till long past midnight in their vacated room, but heard and saw nothing unusual. He states in conclusion that "Randall could not reach that part of the floor from which the rapping came on any occasion without attracting my attention and that of my comrade."

The next case related by Professor Barrett occurred in County Fermanagh, at a spot eleven miles from Enniskillen and about two miles from the hamlet of Derrygonelly, where there dwelt a farmer and his family of four girls and a boy, of whom the eldest was a girl of about twenty years of age named Maggie. His cottage consisted of three rooms, the kitchen, or dwelling-room, being in the centre, with a room on each side used as bedrooms. In one of these two rooms Maggie slept with her sisters, and it was here that the disturbances occurred, generally after they had all gone to bed, when rappings and scratchings were heard which often lasted all night. Rats were first blamed, but when things were moved by some unseen agent, and boots and candles thrown out of the house, it was seen that something more than the ordinary rat was at work. The old farmer, who was a Methodist, sought advice from his class leader, and by his directions laid an open Bible on the bed in the haunted room, placing a big stone on the book. But the stone was lifted off by an unseen hand, the Bible moved out of the room, and seventeen pages torn out of it. They could not keep a lamp or candle in the house, so they went to their neighbours for help, and, to quote the old farmer's words to Professor Barrett, "Jack Flanigan came and lent us a lamp, saying the devil himself would not steal it, as he had got the priest to sprinkle it with holy water." "But that," the old man said, "did us no good either, for the next day it took away that lamp also."

Professor Barrett, at the invitation of Mr. Thomas Plunkett of Enniskillen, went to investigate. He got a full account from the farmer of the freakish tricks which were continually being played in the house, and gives a graphic account of what he himself observed: "After the children, except the boy, had gone to bed, Maggie lay down on the bed without undressing, so that her hands and feet could be observed. The rest of us sat round the kitchen fire, when faint raps, rapidly increasing in loudness, were heard coming apparently from the walls, the ceiling, and various parts of the inner room, the door of which was open. On entering the bedroom with a light the noises at first ceased, but recommenced when I put the light on the window-sill in the kitchen. I had the boy and his father by my side, and asked Mr. Plunkett to look round the house outside. Standing in the doorway leading to the bedroom, the noises recommenced, the light was gradually brought nearer, and after much patience I was able to bring the light into the bedroom whilst the disturbances were still loudly going on. At last I was able to go up to the side of the bed, with the lighted candle in my hand, and closely observed each of the occupants lying on the bed. The younger children were apparently asleep, and Maggie was motionless; nevertheless, knocks were going on everywhere around; on the chairs, the bedstead, the walls and ceiling. The closest scrutiny failed to detect any movement on the part of those present that could account for the noises, which were accompanied by a scratching or tearing sound. Suddenly a large pebble fell in my presence on to the bed; no one had moved to dislodge it, even if it had been placed for the purpose. When I replaced the candle on the window-sill in the kitchen, the knocks became still louder, like those made by a heavy carpenter's hammer driving nails into flooring."

A couple of days afterwards, the Rev. Maxwell Close, M.A., a well-known member of the S.P.R., joined Professor Barrett and Mr. Plunkett, and together the party of three paid visits on two consecutive nights to the haunted farm-house, and the noises were repeated. Complete search was made, both inside and outside of the house, but no cause could be found. When the party were leaving, the old farmer was much perturbed that they had not "laid the ghost." When questioned he said he thought it was fairies. He was asked if it had answered to questions by raps and he said he had; "but it tells lies as often as truth, and oftener, I think. We tried it, and it only knocked at L M N when we said the alphabet over." Professor Barrett then tested it by asking mentally for a certain number of raps, and immediately the actual number was heard. He repeated this four times with a different number each time, and with the same result.

Perhaps the most interesting part of this particular case is at the end of Professor Barrett's account, when, at the request of the old farmer, Mr. Maxwell Close read some passages from Scripture, followed by the Lord's Prayer, to an accompaniment of knockings and scratches, which were at first so loud that the solemn words could hardly be heard, but which gradually ceased as they all knelt in prayer. And since that night no further disturbance occurred.

Another similar story comes from the north of Ireland. In the year 1866 (as recorded in the *Larne Reporter* of March 31 in that year), two families residing at Upper Ballygowan, near Larne, suffered a series of annoyances from having stones thrown into their houses both by night and by day. Their neighbours came in great numbers to sympathise with them in their affliction, and on one occasion, after a volley of stones had been poured into the house through the window, a young man who was present fired a musket in the direction of the mysterious assailants. The reply was a loud peal of satanic laughter, followed by a volley of stones and turf. On another occasion a heap of potatoes, which was in an inner apartment of one of the houses, was seen to be in commotion, and shortly afterwards its contents were hurled into the kitchen, where the inmates of the house, with some of their neighbours, were assembled.

The explanation given by some people of this mysterious affair was as mysterious as the affair itself. It was said that many years before the occurrences which we have now related took place, the farmer who then occupied the premises in which they happened was greatly annoyed by mischievous tricks which were played upon him by a company of fairies who had a habit of holding their rendezvous in his house. The consequence was that this man had to leave the house, which for a long time stood a roofless ruin. After the lapse of many years, and when the story about the dilapidated fabric having been haunted had probably been forgotten, the people who then occupied the adjoining lands unfortunately took some of the stones of the old deserted mansion to repair their own buildings. At this the fairies, or "good people," were much incensed; and they vented their displeasure on the offender in the way we have described.

A correspondent from County Wexford, who desires to have his name suppressed, writes as follows: "Less than ten miles from the town of ———, Co. Wexford, lives a small farmer named M—, who by dint of thrift and industry has reared a large family decently and comfortably.

"Some twenty years ago Mr. M—, through the death of a relative, fell in for a legacy of about a hundred pounds. As he was already in rather prosperous circumstances, and as his old thatched dwelling-house was not large enough to accommodate his increasing family, he resolved to spend the money in building a new one.

"Not long afterwards building operations commenced, and in about a year he had a fine slated cottage, or small farm-house, erected and ready for occupation: so far very well; but it is little our friend M— anticipated the troubles which were still ahead of him. He purchased some new furniture at the nearest town, and on a certain day he removed all the furniture which the old house contained into the new one; and in the evening the family found themselves installed in the latter for good, as they thought. They all retired to rest at their usual hour; scarcely were they snugly settled in bed when they heard peculiar noises inside the house. As time passed the din became terrible—there was shuffling of feet, slamming of doors, pulling about of furniture, and so forth. The man of the house got up to explore, but could see nothing, neither was anything disturbed. The door was securely locked as he had left it. After a thorough investigation, in which his wife assisted, he had to own he could find no clue to the cause of the disturbance. The couple went to bed again, and almost immediately the racket recommenced, and continued more or less till dawn.

"The inmates were puzzled and frightened, but determined to try whether the noise would be repeated the next night before telling their neighbours what had happened. But the pandemonium experienced the first night of their occupation was as nothing compared with what they had to endure the second night and for several succeeding nights. Sleep was impossible, and finally Mr. M— and family in terror abandoned their new home, and retook possession of their old one.

"That is the state of things to this day. The old house has been repaired and is tenanted. The new house, a few perches off, facing the public road, is used as a storehouse. The writer has seen it scores of times, and its story is well known all over the countryside. Mr. M— is disinclined to discuss the matter or to answer questions; but it is said he made several subsequent attempts to occupy the house, but always failed to stand his ground when night came with its usual rowdy disturbances.

"It is said that when building operations were about to begin, a little man of bizarre appearance accosted Mr. M— and exhorted him to build on a different site; otherwise the consequences would be unpleasant for him and his; while the local peasantry allege that the house was built across a fairy pathway between two *raths*, and that this was the cause of the trouble. It is quite true that there are two large *raths* in the vicinity, and the haunted house is directly in a bee-line between them. For myself I offer no explanation; but I guarantee the substantial accuracy of what I have stated above."

Professor Barrett, in the paper to which we have already referred, draws certain conclusions from his study of this subject; one of the chief of these is that "the widespread belief in fairies, pixies, gnomes, brownies, &c., probably rests on the varied manifestations of poltergeists." The popular explanation of the above story bears out this conclusion, and it is further emphasized by the following, which comes from Portarlington:

A man near that town had saved five hundred pounds, and determined to build a house with the money. He fixed on a certain spot, and began to build, very much against the advice of his friends, who said it was on a fairy path, and would bring him ill-luck. Soon the house was finished, and the owner moved in; but the very first night his troubles began, for some unseen hand threw the furniture about and broke it, while the man himself was injured. Being unwilling to lose the value of his money, he tried to make the best of things. But night after night the disturbances continued, and life in the house was impossible; the owner chose the better part of valour and left. No tenant has been found since, and the house stands empty, a silent testimony to the power of the poltergeist.

Poltergeistic phenomena from their very nature lend themselves to spurious reproduction and imitation, as witness the famous case of Cock Lane and many other similar stories. At least one well-known case occurred in Ireland, and is interesting as showing that where fraud is at work, close investigation will discover it. It is related that an old Royal Irish Constabulary pensioner, who obtained a post as emergency man during the land troubles, and who in 1892 was in charge of an evicted farm in the Passage East district, was being continually disturbed by furniture and crockery being thrown about in a mysterious manner. Reports were brought to the police, and they investigated the matter; but nothing was heard or seen beyond knocking on an inside wall of a bedroom in which one of the sons was sleeping; this knocking ceased when the police were in the bedroom, and no search was made in the boy's bed to see if he had a stick. The police therefore could find no explanation, the noises continued night after night, and eventually the family left and went to live in Waterford. A great furore was raised when it was learnt that the hauntings had followed them, and again investigation was made, but it seems to have been more careful this time: an eye was kept on the movements of the young son, and at least two independent witnesses saw him throwing things about— fireirons and jam-pots—when he thought his father was not looking. It seems to have been a plot between the mother and son owing to the former's dislike to her husband's occupation, which entailed great unpopularity and considerable personal risk. Fearing for her own and her family's safety, the wife conceived of this plan to force her husband to give up his post. Her efforts were successful, as the man soon resigned his position and went to live elsewhere.

CHAPTER V

Haunted Places

THAT HOUSES ARE haunted and apparitions frequently seen therein are pretty well established facts. The preceding chapters have dealt with this aspect of the subject, and, in view of the weight of evidence to prove the truth of the stories told in them, it would be hard for anyone to doubt that there is such a thing as a haunted house, whatever explanation may be given of "haunting." We now turn to another division of the subject—the outdoor ghost who haunts the roadways, country lanes, and other places. Sceptics on ghostly phenomena are generally pretty full of explanations when they are told of a ghost having been seen in a particular spot, and the teller may be put down as hyper-imaginative, or as having been deluded by moonlight playing through the trees; while cases are not wanting where a reputation for temperance has been lost by a man telling his experiences of a ghost he happens to have met along some country lane; and the fact that there are cases where an imaginative and nervous person has mistaken for a ghost a white goat or a sheet hanging on a bush only strengthens the sceptic's disbelief and makes him blind to the very large weight of evidence that can be arrayed against him. Some day, no doubt, psychologists and scientists will be able to give us a complete and satisfactory explanation of these abnormal apparitions, but at present we are very much in the dark, and any explanation that may be put forward is necessarily of a tentative nature.

The following story is sent us by Mr. J. J. Crowley, of the Munster and Leinster Bank, who writes as follows: "The scene is outside Clonmel, on the main road leading up to a nice old residence on the side of the mountains called —— Lodge. I happened to be visiting my friends, two other bank men. It was night, about eight o'clock, moonless, and tolerably dark, and when within a quarter of a mile or perhaps less of a bridge over a small stream near the house I saw a girl, dressed in white, wearing a black sash and long flowing hair, walk in the direction from me up the culvert of the bridge and disappear down the other side. At the time I saw it I thought it most peculiar that I could distinguish a figure so far away, and thought a light of some sort must be falling on the girl, or that there were some people about and that some of them had struck a match. When I got to the place I looked about, but could find no person there.

"I related this story to my friends some time after arriving, and was then told that one of them had wakened up in his sleep a few nights previously, and had seen an identical figure standing at the foot of his bed, and rushed in fright from his room, taking refuge for the night with the other lodger. They told the story to their landlady, and learned from her that this apparition had frequently been seen about the place, and was the spirit of one of her daughters who had died years previously rather young, and who, previous to her death, had gone about just as we described the figure we had seen. I had heard nothing of this story until after I had seen the ghost, and consequently it could not be put down to hallucination or over-imagination on my part."

The experiences of two constables of the Royal Irish Constabulary while on despatch duty one winter's night in the early eighties has been sent us by one of the men concerned, and provides interesting reading. It was a fine moonlight night, with a touch of frost in the air, when these two men set out to march the five miles to the next barrack. Brisk walking soon brought them near their destination. The barrack which they were approaching was on the left side of the road, and facing it on the other side was a white-thorn hedge. The road at this point was wide, and as the two constables got within fifty yards of the barrack, they saw a policeman step out from this hedge and move across the road, looking towards the two men as he did so. He was plainly visible to them both. "He was bare-headed" (runs the account), "with his tunic opened down the front, a stout-built man, black-haired, pale, full face, and short mutton-chop whiskers." They thought he was a newly-joined constable who was doing "guard" and had come out to get some fresh air while waiting for a patrol to return. As the two men approached, he disappeared into the shadow of the barrack, and apparently went in by the door; to their amazement, when they came up they found the door closed and bolted, and it was only after loud knocking that they got a sleepy "All right" from some one inside, and after the usual challenging were admitted. There was no sign of the strange policeman when they got in, and on inquiry they learnt that no new constable had joined the station. The two men realised then that they had seen a ghost, but refrained from saying anything about it to the men at the station—a very sensible precaution, considering the loneliness of the average policeman's life in this country.

Some years afterwards the narrator of the above story learnt that a policeman had been lost in a snow-drift near this particular barrack. Whether this be the explanation we leave to others: the facts as stated are well vouched for. There is no evidence to support the theory of hallucination, for the apparition was so vivid that the idea of its being other than normal never entered the constables' heads *till they had got into the barrack.* When they found the door shut and bolted, their amazement was caused by indignation against an apparently unsociable or thoughtless comrade, and it was only afterwards, while discussing the whole thing on their homeward journey, that it occurred to them that it would have been impossible for any ordinary mortal to shut, bolt, and bar a door without making a sound.

In the winter of 1840-1, in the days when snow and ice and all their attendant pleasures were more often in evidence than in these degenerate days, a skating party was enjoying itself on the pond in the grounds of the Castle near Rathfarnham, Co. Dublin. Among the skaters was a man who had with him a very fine curly-coated retriever dog. The pond was thronged with people enjoying themselves, when suddenly the ice gave way beneath him, and the man fell into the water; the dog went to his rescue, and both were drowned. A monument was erected to perpetuate the memory of the dog's heroic self-sacrifice, but only the pedestal now remains. The ghost of the dog is said to haunt the grounds and the public road between the castle gate and the Dodder Bridge. Many people have seen the phantom dog, and the story is well known locally.

The ghost of a boy who was murdered by a Romany is said to haunt one of the lodge gates of the Castle demesne, and the lodge-keeper states that he saw it only a short time ago. The Castle, however, is now in possession of Jesuit Fathers, and the Superior assures us that there has been no sign of a ghost for a long time, his explanation being that the place is so crowded out with new buildings "that even a ghost would have some difficulty in finding a comfortable corner."

It is a fairly general belief amongst students of supernatural phenomena that animals have the psychic faculty developed to a greater extent than we have. There are numerous stories which tell of animals being scared and frightened by something that is invisible to a human being, and the explanation given is that the animal has seen a ghost which we cannot see. A story that is told of a certain spot near the village of G—, in Co. Kilkenny, supports this theory. The account was sent us by the eye-witness of what occurred, and runs as follows: "I was out for a walk one evening near the town of G— about 8.45 P.M., and was crossing the bridge that leads into the S. Carlow district with a small wire-haired terrier dog. When we were about three-quarters of a mile out, the dog began to bark and yelp in a most vicious manner at 'nothing' on the left-hand side of the roadway and near to a straggling hedge. I felt a bit creepy and that something was wrong. The dog kept on barking, but I could at first see nothing, but on looking closely for a few seconds I believe I saw a small grey-white object vanish gradually and noiselessly into the hedge. No sooner had it vanished than the dog ceased barking, wagged his tail, and seemed pleased with his successful efforts." The narrator goes on to say that he made inquiries when he got home, and found that this spot on the road had a very bad reputation, as people had frequently seen a ghost there, while horses had often to be beaten, coaxed, or led past the place. The explanation locally current is that a suicide was buried at the cross-roads near at hand, or that it may be the ghost of a man who is known to have been killed at the spot.

The following story has been sent us by the Rev. H. R. B. Gillespie, to whom it was told by one of the witnesses of the incidents described therein. One bright moonlight night some time ago a party consisting of a man, his two daughters, and a friend were driving along a country road in County Leitrim. They came to a steep hill, and all except the driver got down to walk. One of the two sisters walked on in front, and after her came the other two, followed closely by the trap. They had not gone far, when those in rear saw a shabbily-dressed man walking beside the girl who was leading. But she did not seem to be taking any notice of him, and, wondering what he could be, they hastened to overtake her. But just when they were catching her up the figure suddenly dashed into the shadow of a disused forge, which stood by the side of the road, and as it did so the horse, which up to this had been perfectly quiet, reared up and became unmanageable. The girl beside whom the figure had walked had seen and heard nothing. The road was not bordered by trees or a high hedge, so that it could not have been some trick of the moonlight. One of the girls described the appearance of the figure to a local workman, who said, "It is very like a tinker who was found dead in that forge about six months ago."

Here is another story of a haunted spot on a road, where a "ghost" was seen, not at the witching hour of night, not when evening shadows lengthen, but in broad daylight. It is sent to us by the percipient, a lady, who does not desire to have her name mentioned. She was walking along a country road in the vicinity of Cork one afternoon, and passed various people. She then saw coming towards her a country-woman dressed in an old-fashioned style. This figure approached her, and when it drew near, suddenly staggered, as if under the influence of drink, and disappeared! She hastened to the spot, but searched in vain for any clue to the mystery; the road was bounded by high walls, and there was no gateway or gap through which the figure might slip. Much mystified, she continued on her way, and arrived at her destination. She there mentioned what had occurred, and was then informed by an old resident in the neighbourhood that that woman had constantly been seen up to twenty years before, but not since that date. By the country-people the road was believed to be haunted, but the percipient did not know this at the time.

The following is sent us by Mr. T. J. Westropp, and has points of its own which are interesting; he states: "On the road from Bray to Windgates, at the Deerpark of Kilruddy, is a spot which, whatever be the explanation, is distinguished by weird sounds and (some say) sights. I on one occasion was walking with a friend to catch the train at Bray about eleven o'clock one evening some twenty-five years ago, when we both heard heavy steps and rustling of bracken in the Deerpark; apparently some one got over the gate, crossed the road with heavy steps and fell from the wall next Bray Head, rustling and slightly groaning. The night was lightsome, though without actual moonlight, and we could see nothing over the wall where we had heard the noise.

"For several years after I dismissed the matter as a delusion; but when I told the story to some cousins, they said that another relative (now a Fellow of Trinity College, Dublin) had heard it too, and that there was a local belief that it was the ghost of a poacher mortally wounded by gamekeepers, who escaped across the road and died beyond it." Mr. Westropp afterwards got the relative mentioned above to tell his experience, and it corresponded with his own, except that the ghost was visible. "The clergyman who was rector of Greystones at that time used to say that he had heard exactly similar noises though he had seen nothing."

The following story of an occurrence near Dublin is sent us by a lady who is a very firm believer in ghosts. On a fine night some years ago two sisters were returning home from the theatre. They were walking along a very lonely part of the Kimmage Road about two miles beyond the tram terminus, and were chatting gaily as they went, when suddenly they heard the "clink, clink" of a chain coming towards them. At first they thought it was a goat or a donkey which had got loose, and was dragging its chain along the ground. But they could see nothing, and could hear no noise but the clink of the chain, although the road was clear and straight. Nearer and nearer came the noise, gradually getting louder, and as it passed them closely they distinctly felt a blast or whiff of air. They were paralysed with an indefinable fear, and were scarcely able to drag themselves along the remaining quarter of a mile to their house. The elder of the two was in very bad health, and the other had almost to carry her. Immediately she entered the house she collapsed, and had to be revived with brandy.

An old woman, it seems, had been murdered for her savings by a tramp near the spot where this strange occurrence took place, and it is thought that there is a connection between the crime and the haunting of this part of the Kimmage Road. Whatever the explanation may be, the whole story bears every evidence of truth, and it would be hard for anyone to disprove it.

Churchyards are generally considered to be the hunting-ground of all sorts and conditions of ghosts. People who would on all other occasions, when the necessity arises, prove themselves to be possessed of at any rate a normal amount of courage, turn pale and shiver at the thought of having to pass through a churchyard at dead of night. It may be some encouragement to such to state that out of a fairly large collection of accounts of haunted places, only one relates to a churchyard. The story is told by Mr. G. H. Millar of Edgeworthstown: "During the winter of 1875," he writes, "I attended a soirée about five miles from here. I was riding, and on my way home about 11:30 P.M. I had to pass by the old ruins and burial-ground of Abbeyshrule. The road led round by two sides of the churchyard. It was a bright moonlight night, and as my girth broke I was walking the horse quite slowly. As I passed the ruin, I saw what I took to be a policeman in a long overcoat; he was walking from the centre of the churchyard towards the corner, and, as far as I could see, would be at the corner by the time I would reach it, and we would meet. Quite suddenly, however, he disappeared, and I could see no trace of him. Soon after I overtook a man who had left the meeting long before me. I expressed wonder that he had not been farther on, and he explained that he went a 'roundabout' way to avoid passing the old abbey, as he did not want to see 'The Monk.' On questioning him, he told me that a monk was often seen in the churchyard."

A story told of a ghost which haunts a certain spot on an estate near the city of Waterford, bears a certain resemblance to the last story for the reason that it was only after the encounter had taken place in both cases that it was known that anything out of the ordinary had been seen. In the early eighties of last century ——— Court, near Waterford, was occupied by Mr. and Mrs. S— and their family of two young boys and a girl of twenty-one years of age. Below the house is a marshy glen with a big open drain cut through it. Late one evening the daughter was out shooting rabbits near this drain and saw, as she thought, her half-brother standing by the drain in a sailor suit, which like other small boys he wore. She called to him once or twice, and to her surprise got no reply. She went towards him, and when she got close he suddenly disappeared. The next day she asked an old dependent, who had lived many years in the place, if there was anything curious about the glen. He replied at once: "Oh! you mean the little sailor man. Sure, he won't do you any harm." This was the first she had heard of anything of the sort, but it was then found that none of the country-people would go through the glen after dusk.

Some time afterwards two sons of the clergyman of the parish in which ——— Court stands were out one evening fishing in the drain, when one of them suddenly said, "What's that sailor doing there?" The other saw nothing, and presently the figure vanished. At the time of the appearance neither had heard of Miss S—'s experience, and no one has been able to explain it, as there is apparently no tradition of any "little sailor man" having been there in the flesh.

Mr. Joseph M'Crossan, a journalist on the staff of the *Strabane Chronicle*, has sent us a cutting from that paper describing a ghost which appeared to men working in an engine-house at Strabane railway station on two successive nights in October 1913. The article depicts very graphically the antics of the ghost and the fear of the men who saw it. Mr. M'Crossan interviewed one of these men (Pinkerton by name), and the story as told in his words is as follows: "Michael Madden, Fred Oliphant, and I were engaged inside a shed cleaning engines, when, at half-past twelve (midnight), a knocking came to all the doors, and continued without interruption, accompanied by unearthly yells. The three of us went to one of the doors, and saw—I could swear to it without doubt—the form of a man of heavy build. I thought I was about to faint. My hair stood high on my head. We all squealed for help, when the watchman and signalman came fast to our aid. Armed with a crowbar, the signalman made a dash at the 'spirit,' but was unable to strike down the ghost, which hovered about our shed till half-past two. It was moonlight, and we saw it plainly. There was no imagination on our part. We three cleaners climbed up the engine, and hid on the roof of the engine, lying there till morning at our wit's end. The next night it came at half-past one. Oliphant approached the spirit within two yards, but he then collapsed, the ghost uttering terrible yells. I commenced work, but the spirit 'gazed' into my face, and I fell forward against the engine. Seven of us saw the ghost this time. Our clothes and everything in the shed were tossed and thrown about."

The other engine-cleaners were interviewed and corroborated Pinkerton's account. One of them stated that he saw the ghost run up and down a ladder leading to a water tank and disappear into it, while the signalman described how he struck at the ghost with a crowbar, but the weapon seemed to go through it. The spirit finally took his departure through the window.

The details of this affair are very much on the lines of the good old-fashioned ghost yarns. But it is hard to see how so many men could labour under the same delusion. The suggestion that the whole thing was a practical joke may also be dismissed, for if the apparition had flesh and bones the crowbar would have soon proved it. The story goes that a man was murdered near the spot some time ago; whether there is any connection between this crime and the apparition it would be hard to say. However, we are not concerned with explanations (for who, as yet, can explain the supernatural?); the facts as stated have all the appearance of truth.

Mr. Patrick Ryan, of P—, Co. Limerick, gives us two stories as he heard them related by Mr. Michael O'Dwyer of the same place. The former is evidently a very strong believer in supernatural phenomena, but he realises how strong is the unbelief of many, and in support of his stories he gives names of several persons who will vouch for the truth of them. With a few alterations, we give the story in his own words: "Mr. O'Dwyer has related how one night, after he had carried the mails to the train, he went with some fodder for a heifer in a field close to the railway station near to which was a creamery. He discovered the animal grazing near the creamery although how she came to be there was a mystery, as a broad trench separated it from the rest of the field, which is only spanned by a plank used by pedestrians when crossing the field. 'Perhaps,' he said in explanation, 'it was that he *should* go there to hear.' It was about a quarter to twelve (midnight), and, having searched the field in vain, he was returning home, when, as he crossed the plank, he espied the heifer browsing peacefully in the aforementioned part of the field which was near the creamery. He gave her the fodder and— Heavens! was he suffering from delusions? Surely his ears were not deceiving him—from the creamery funnel there arose a dense volume of smoke mingled with the sharp hissing of steam and the rattling of cans, all as if the creamery were working, and it were broad daylight. His heifer became startled and bellowed frantically. O'Dwyer, himself a man of nerves, yet possessing all the superstitions of the Celt, was startled and ran without ceasing to his home near by, where he went quickly to bed.

"O'Dwyer is not the only one who has seen this, as I have been told by several of my friends how they heard it. Who knows the mystery surrounding this affair!"

77

The second story relates to a certain railway station in the south of Ireland; again we use Mr. Ryan's own words: "A near relative of mine" (he writes) "once had occasion to go to the mail train to meet a friend. While sitting talking to O'Dwyer, whom he met on the platform, he heard talking going on in the waiting-room. O'Dwyer heard it also, and they went to the door, but saw nothing save for the light of a waning moon which filtered in through the window. Uncertain, they struck matches, but saw nothing. Again they sat outside, and again they heard the talking, and this time they did not go to look, for they knew about it. In the memory of the writer a certain unfortunate person committed suicide on the railway, and was carried to the waiting-room pending an inquest. He lay all night there till the inquest was held next day. 'Let us not look further into the matter,' said O'Dwyer, and my relative having acquiesced, he breathed a shuddering prayer for the repose of the dead."

The following story, which has been sent as a personal experience by Mr. William Mackey of Strabane, is similar in many ways to an extraordinary case of retro-cognitive vision which occurred some years ago to two English ladies who were paying a visit to Versailles; and who published their experiences in a book entitled, *An Adventure* (London, 1911). Mr. Mackey writes: "It was during the severe winter of the Crimean War, when indulging in my favourite sport of wild-fowl shooting, that I witnessed the following strange scene. It was a bitterly cold night towards the end of November or beginning of December; the silvery moon had sunk in the west shortly before midnight; the sport had been all that could be desired, when I began to realise that the blood was frozen in my veins, and I was on the point of starting for home, when my attention was drawn to the barking of a dog close by, which was followed in a few seconds by the loud report of a musket, the echo of which had scarcely died away in the silent night, when several musket-shots went off in quick succession; this seemed to be the signal for a regular fusillade of musketry, and it was quite evident from the nature of the firing that there was attack and defence.

"For the life of me I could not understand what it all meant; not being superstitious I did not for a moment imagine it was supernatural, notwithstanding that my courageous dog was crouching in abject terror between my legs; beads of perspiration began to trickle down from my forehead, when suddenly there arose a flame as if a house were on fire, but I knew from the position of the blaze (which was only a few hundred yards from where I stood), that there was no house there, or any combustible that would burn, and what perplexed me most was to see pieces of burning thatch and timber sparks fall hissing into the water at my feet. When the fire seemed at its height the firing appeared to weaken, and when the clear sound of a bugle floated out on the midnight air, it suddenly ceased, and I could hear distinctly the sound of cavalry coming at a canter, their accoutrements jingling quite plainly on the frosty air; in a very short time they arrived at the scene of the fight. I thought it an eternity until they took their departure, which they did at the walk.

"It is needless to say that, although the scene of this tumult was on my nearest way home, I did not venture that way, as, although there are many people who would say that I never knew what fear was, I must confess on this occasion I was thoroughly frightened.

"At breakfast I got a good sound rating from my father for staying out so late. My excuse was that I fell asleep and had a horrible dream, which I related. When I finished I was told I had been dreaming with my eyes open!—that I was not the first person who had witnessed this strange sight. He then told me the following narrative: 'It was towards the end of the seventeenth century that a widow named Sally Mackey and her three sons lived on the outskirts of the little settlement of the Mackeys. A warrant was issued by the Government against the three sons for high treason, the warrant being delivered for execution to the officer in command of the infantry regiment stationed at Lifford. A company was told off for the purpose of effecting the arrest, and the troops set out from Lifford at 11 P.M.

"'The cottage home of the Mackeys was approached by a bridle-path, leading from the main road to Derry, which only permitted the military to approach in single file; they arrived there at midnight, and the first intimation the inmates had of danger was the barking, and then the shooting, of the collie dog. Possessing as they did several stand of arms, they opened fire on the soldiers as they came in view and killed and wounded several; it was the mother, Sally Mackey, who did the shooting, the sons loading the muskets. Whether the cottage went on fire by accident or design was never known; it was only when the firing from the cottage ceased and the door was forced open that the officer in command rushed in and brought out the prostrate form of the lady, who was severely wounded and burned. All the sons perished, but the soldiers suffered severely, a good many being killed and wounded.

"'The firing was heard by the sentries at Lifford, and a troop of cavalry was despatched to the scene of conflict, but only arrived in time to see the heroine dragged from the burning cottage. She had not, however, been fatally wounded, and lived for many years afterwards with a kinsmen. My father remembered conversing with old men, when he was a boy, who remembered her well. She seemed to take a delight in narrating incidents of the fight to those who came to visit her, and would always finish up by making them feel the pellets between the skin and her ribs.'"

CHAPTER VI
Apparitions at or After Death

It HAS BEEN said by a very eminent literary man that the accounts of the appearance of people at or shortly after the moment of death make very dull reading as a general rule. This may be; they are certainly not so lengthy, or full of detail, as the accounts of haunted houses—nor could such be expected. In our humble opinion, however, they are full of interest, and open up problems of telepathy and thought-transference to which the solutions may not be found for years to come. That people have seen the image of a friend or relative at the moment of dissolution, sometimes in the ordinary garb of life, sometimes with symbolical accompaniments, or that they have been made acquainted in some abnormal manner with the fact that such a one has passed away, seems to be demonstrated beyond all reasonable doubt. But we would hasten to add that such appearances are not a proof of existence after death, nor can they be regarded in the light of special interventions of a merciful Providence. Were they either they would surely occur far oftener. The question is, Why do they occur at all? As it is, the majority of them seem to happen for no particular reason, and are often seen by persons who have little or no connection with the deceased, not by their nearest and dearest, as one might expect. It is supposed they are *veridical* hallucinations, *i.e.* ones which correspond with objective events at a distance, and are caused by a telepathic impact conveyed from the mind of an absent agent to the mind of the percipient.

From their nature they fall under different heads. The majority of them occur at what may most conveniently be described as the time of death, though how closely they approximate in reality to the instant of the Great Change it is impossible to say. So we have divided this chapter into three groups:

(1) Appearances at the time of death (as explained above).

(2) Appearances clearly *after* the time of death.

(3) In this third group we hope to give three curious tales of appearances some time *before* death.

Group I

We commence this group with stories in which the phenomena connected with the respective deaths were not perceived as representations of the human form. In the first only sounds were heard. It is sent as a personal experience by the Archdeacon of Limerick, Very Rev. J. A. Haydn, LL.D. "In the year 1879 there lived in the picturesque village of Adare, at a distance of about eight or nine miles from my residence, a District Inspector named ——, with whom I enjoyed a friendship of the most intimate and fraternal kind. At the time I write of, Mrs. —— was expecting the arrival of their third child. She was a particularly tiny and fragile woman, and much anxiety was felt as to the result of the impending event. He and she had very frequently spent pleasant days at my house, with all the apartments of which they were thoroughly acquainted—a fact of importance in this narrative.

"On Wednesday, October 17, 1879, I had a very jubilant letter from my friend, announcing that the expected event had successfully happened on the previous day, and that all was progressing satisfactorily. On the night of the following Wednesday, I retired to bed at about ten o'clock. My wife, the children, and two maid-servants were all sleeping upstairs, and I had a small bed in my study, which was on the ground floor. The house was shrouded in darkness, and the only sound that broke the silence was the ticking of the hall-clock.

"I was quietly preparing to go to sleep, when I was much surprised at hearing, with the most unquestionable distinctness, the sound of light, hurried footsteps, exactly suggestive of those of an active, restless young female, coming in from the hall door and traversing the hall. They then, apparently with some hesitation, followed the passage leading to the study door, on arriving at which they stopped. I then heard the sound of a light, agitated hand apparently searching for the handle of the door. By this time, being quite sure that my wife had come down and wanted to speak to me, I sat up in bed, and called to her by name, asking what was the matter. As there was no reply, and the sounds had ceased, I struck a match, lighted a candle, and opened the door. No one was visible or audible. I went upstairs, found all the doors shut and everyone asleep. Greatly puzzled, I returned to the study and went to bed, leaving the candle alight. Immediately the whole performance was circumstantially repeated, but *this* time the handle of the door was grasped by the invisible hand, and *partly* turned, then relinquished. I started out of bed and renewed my previous search, with equally futile results. The clock struck eleven, and from that time all disturbances ceased.

"On Friday morning I received a letter stating that Mrs. ———— had died at about midnight on the previous Wednesday. I hastened off to Adare and had an interview with my bereaved friend. With one item of our conversation I will close. He told me that his wife sank rapidly on Wednesday, until when night came on she became delirious. She spoke incoherently, as if revisiting scenes and places once familiar. 'She thought she was in *your* house,' he said, 'and was apparently holding a conversation with *you*, as she used to keep silence at intervals as if listening to your replies.' I asked him if he could possibly remember the hour at which the imaginary conversation took place. He replied that, curiously enough, he could tell it accurately, as he had looked at his watch, and found the time between half-past ten and eleven o'clock—the exact time of the mysterious manifestations heard by me."

A lady sends the following personal experience: "I had a cousin in the country who was not very strong, and on one occasion she desired me to go to her, and accompany her to K—. I consented to do so, and arranged a day to go and meet her: this was in the month of February. The evening before I was to go, I was sitting by the fire in my small parlour about 5 P.M. There was no light in the room except what proceeded from the fire. Beside the fire-place was an armchair, where my cousin usually sat when she was with me. Suddenly that chair was illuminated by a light so intensely bright that it actually seemed to *heave* under it, though the remainder of the room remained in semi-darkness. I called out in amazement, 'What has happened to the chair?' In a moment the light vanished, and the chair was as before. In the morning I heard that my cousin had died about the same time that I saw the light."

We now come to the ordinary type, *i.e.* where a figure appears. The following tale illustrates a point we have already alluded to, namely, that the apparition is sometimes seen by a disinterested person, and *not* by those whom one would naturally expect should see it. A lady writes as follows: "At Island Magee is the Knowehead Lonan, a long, hilly, narrow road, bordered on either side by high thorn-hedges and fields. Twenty years ago, when I was a young girl, I used to go to the post-office at the Knowehead on Sunday mornings down the Lonan, taking the dogs for the run. One Sunday as I had got to the top of the hill on my return journey, I looked back, and saw a man walking rapidly after me, but still a good way off. I hastened my steps, for the day was muddy, and I did not want him to see me in a bedraggled state. But he seemed to come on so fast as to be soon close behind me, and I wondered he did not pass me, so on we went, I never turning to look back. About a quarter of a mile farther on I met A. B. on 'Dick's Brae,' on her way to church or Sunday school, and stopped to speak to her. I wanted to ask who the man was, but he seemed to be so close that I did not like to do so, and expected he had passed. When I moved on, I was surprised to find he was still following me, while my dogs were lagging behind with downcast heads and drooping tails.

"I then passed a cottage where C. D. was out feeding her fowls. I spoke to her, and then feeling that there was no longer anyone behind, looked back, and saw the man standing with her. I would not have paid any attention to the matter had not A. B. been down at our house that afternoon, and I casually asked her:

"'Who was the man who was just behind me when I met you on Dick's Brae?'

"'What man?' said she; and noting my look of utter astonishment, added, 'I give you my word I never met a soul but yourself from the time I left home till I went down to Knowehead Lonan.'

"Next day C. D. came to work for us, and I asked her who was the man who was standing beside her after I passed her on Sunday.

"'Naebody!' she replied, 'I saw naebody but yoursel'.'

"It all seemed very strange, and so they thought too. About three weeks later news came that C. D.'s only brother, a sailor, was washed overboard that Sunday morning."

The following story is not a first-hand experience, but is sent by the gentleman to whom it was related by the percipient. The latter said to him:

"I was sitting in this same chair I am in at present one evening, when I heard a knock at the front door. I went myself to see who was there, and on opening the door saw my old friend P. Q. standing outside with his gun in his hand. I was surprised at seeing him, but asked him to come in and have something. He came inside the porch into the lamplight, and stood there for a few moments; then he muttered something about being sorry he had disturbed me, and that he was on his way to see his brother, Colonel Q., who lived about a mile farther on. Without any further explanation he walked away towards the gate into the dusk.

"I was greatly surprised and perplexed, but as he had gone I sat down again by the fire. About an hour later another knock came to the door, and I again went out to see who was there. On opening it I found P. Q.'s groom holding a horse, and he asked me where he was, as he had missed his way in the dark, and did not know the locality. I told him, and then asked him where he was going, and why, and he replied that his master was dead (at his own house about nine miles away), and that he had been sent to announce the news to Colonel Q."

Miss Grene, of Grene Park, Co. Tipperary, relates a story which was told her by the late Miss ———, sister of a former Dean of Cashel. The latter, an old lady, stated that one time she was staying with a friend in a house in the suburbs of Dublin. In front of the house was the usual grass plot, divided into two by a short gravel path which led down to a gate which opened on to the street. She and her friend were one day engaged in needlework in one of the front rooms, when they heard the gate opening, and on looking out the window they saw an elderly gentleman of their acquaintance coming up the path. As he approached the door both exclaimed: "Oh, how good of him to come and see us!" As he was not shown into the sitting-room, one of them rang the bell, and said to the maid when she appeared, "You have not let Mr. So-and-so in; he is at the door for some little time." The maid went to the hall door, and returned to say that there was no one there. Next day they learnt that he had died just at the hour that they had seen him coming up the path.

The following tale contains a curious point. A good many years ago the Rev. Henry Morton, now dead, held a curacy in Ireland. He had to pass through the graveyard when leaving his house to visit the parishioners. One beautiful moonlight night he was sent for to visit a sick person, and was accompanied by his brother, a medical man, who was staying with him. After performing the religious duty they returned through the churchyard, and were chatting about various matters when to their astonishment a figure passed them, both seeing it. This figure left the path, and went in among the gravestones, and then disappeared. They could not understand this at all, so they went to the spot where the disappearance took place, but, needless to say, could find nobody after the most careful search. Next morning they heard that the person visited had died just after their departure, while the most marvellous thing of all was that the burial took place at the very spot where they had seen the phantom disappear.

The Rev. D. B. Knox communicates the following: In a girls' boarding-school several years ago two of the boarders were sleeping in a large double-bedded room with two doors. About two o'clock in the morning the girls were awakened by the entrance of a tall figure in clerical attire, the face of which they did not see. They screamed in fright, but the figure moved in a slow and stately manner past their beds, and out the other door. It also appeared to one or two of the other boarders, and seemed to be looking for some one. At length it reached the bed of one who was evidently known to it. The girl woke up and recognised her father. He did not speak, but gazed for a few moments at his daughter, and then vanished. Next morning a telegram was handed to her which communicated the sad news that her father had died on the previous evening at the hour when he appeared to her.

Here is a story of a very old type. It occurred a good many years ago. A gentleman named Miller resided in Co. Wexford, while his friend and former schoolfellow lived in the North of Ireland. This long friendship led them to visit at each other's houses from time to time, but for Mr. Miller there was a deep shadow of sorrow over these otherwise happy moments, for, while he enjoyed the most enlightened religious opinions, his friend was an unbeliever. The last time they were together Mr. Scott said, "My dear friend, let us solemnly promise that whichever of us shall die first shall appear to the other after death, if it be possible." "Let it be so, if God will," replied Mr. Miller. One morning some time after, about three o'clock, the latter was awakened by a brilliant light in his bedroom; he imagined that the house must be on fire, when he felt what seemed to be a hand laid on him, and heard his friend's voice say distinctly, "There is a God, just but terrible in His judgments," and all again was dark. Mr. Miller at once wrote down this remarkable experience. Two days later he received a letter announcing Mr. Scott's death on the night, and at the hour, that he had seen the light in his room.

The above leads us on to the famous "Beresford Ghost," which is generally regarded as holding the same position relative to Irish ghosts that Dame Alice Kyteler used to hold with respect to Irish witches and wizards. The story is so well known, and has been published so often, that only a brief allusion is necessary, with the added information that the best version is to be found in Andrew Lang's *Dreams and Ghosts*, chapter viii. (Silver Library Edition). Lord Tyrone appeared after death one night to Lady Beresford at Gill Hall, in accordance with a promise (as in the last story) made in early life. He assured her that the religion as revealed by Jesus Christ was the only true one (both he and Lady Beresford had been brought up Deists), told her that she was *enceinte* and would bear a son, and also foretold her second marriage, and the time of her death. In proof whereof he drew the bed-hangings through an iron hook, wrote his name in her pocket-book, and finally placed a hand cold as marble on her wrist, at which the sinews shrunk up. To the day of her death Lady Beresford wore a black ribbon round her wrist; this was taken off before her burial, and it was found the nerves were withered, and the sinews shrunken, as she had previously described to her children.

Group II

We now come to some stories of apparitions seen some time after the hour of death. Canon Ross-Lewin, of Limerick, furnishes the following incident in his own family. "My uncle, John Dillon Ross-Lewin, lieutenant in the 30th Regiment, was mortally wounded at Inkerman on November 5, 1854, and died on the morning of the 6th. He appeared that night to his mother, who was then on a visit in Co. Limerick, intimating his death, and indicating where the wound was. The strangest part of the occurrence is, that when news came later on of the casualties at Inkerman, the first account as to the wound did *not* correspond with what the apparition indicated to his mother, but the final account did. Mrs. Ross-Lewin was devoted to her son, and he was equally attached to her; she, as the widow of a field officer who fought at Waterloo, would be able to comprehend the battle scene, and her mind at the time was centred on the events of the Crimean War."

A clergyman, who desires that all names be suppressed, sends the following: "In my wife's father's house a number of female servants were kept, of whom my wife, before she was married, was in charge. On one occasion the cook took ill with appendicitis, and was operated on in the Infirmary, where I attended her as hospital chaplain. She died, however, and was buried by her friends. Some days after the funeral my wife was standing at a table in the kitchen which was so placed that any person standing at it could see into the passage outside the kitchen, if the door happened to be open. [The narrator enclosed a rough plan which made the whole story perfectly clear.] She was standing one day by herself at the table, and the door was open. This was in broad daylight, about eleven o'clock in the morning in the end of February or beginning of March. She was icing a cake, and therefore was hardly thinking of ghosts. Suddenly she looked up from her work, and glanced through the open kitchen door into the passage leading past the servants' parlour into the dairy. She saw quite distinctly the figure of the deceased cook pass towards the dairy; she was dressed in the ordinary costume she used to wear in the mornings, and seemed in every respect quite normal. My wife was not, at the moment, in the least shocked or surprised, but on the contrary she followed, and searched in the dairy, into which she was just in time to see her skirts disappearing. Needless to say, nothing was visible."

Canon Courtenay Moore, M.A., Rector of Mitchelstown, contributes a personal experience. "It was about eighteen years ago—I cannot fix the exact date—that Samuel Penrose returned to this parish from the Argentine. He was getting on so well abroad that he would have remained there, but his wife fell ill, and for her sake he returned to Ireland. He was a carpenter by trade, and his former employer was glad to take him into his service again. Sam was a very respectable man of sincere religious feelings. Soon after his return he met with one or two rather severe accidents, and had a strong impression that a fatal one would happen him before long; and so it came to pass. A scaffolding gave way one day, and precipitated him on to a flagged stone floor. He did not die immediately, but his injuries proved fatal. He died in a Cork hospital soon after his admission: I went to Cork to officiate at his funeral. About noon the next day I was standing at my hall door, and the form of poor Sam, the upper half of it, seemed to pass before me. He looked peaceful and happy—it was a momentary vision, but perfectly distinct. The truncated appearance puzzled me very much, until some time after I read a large book by F. W. H. Myers, in which he made a scientific analysis and induction of such phenomena, and said that they were almost universally seen in this half-length form. I do not profess to explain what I saw: its message, if it had a message, seemed to be that poor Sam was at last at rest and in peace."

A story somewhat similar to the above was related to us, in which the apparition seems certainly to have been sent with a definite purpose. Two maiden ladies, whom we shall call Miss A. X. and Miss B. Y., lived together for a good many years. As one would naturally expect, they were close friends, and had the most intimate relations with each other, both being extremely religious women. In process of time Miss B. Y. died, and after death Miss A. X. formed the impression, for some unknown reason, that all was not well with her friend—that, in fact, her soul was not at rest. This thought caused her great uneasiness and trouble of mind. One day she was sitting in her armchair thinking over this, and crying bitterly. Suddenly she saw in front of her a brilliant light, in the midst of which was her friend's face, easily recognisable, but transfigured, and wearing a most beatific expression. She rushed towards it with her arms outstretched, crying, "Oh! B., why have you come?" At this the apparition faded away, but ever after Miss A. X. was perfectly tranquil in mind with respect to her friend's salvation.

This group may be brought to a conclusion by a story sent by Mr. T. MacFadden. It is not a personal experience, but happened to his father, and in an accompanying letter he states that he often heard the latter describe the incidents related therein, and that he certainly saw the ghost.

"The island of Inishinny, which is the scene of this story, is one of the most picturesque islands on the Donegal coast. With the islands of Gola and Inismaan it forms a perfectly natural harbour and safe anchorage for ships during storms. About Christmas some forty or fifty years ago a small sailing-ship put into Gola Roads (as this anchorage is called) during a prolonged storm, and the captain and two men had to obtain provisions from Bunbeg, as, owing to their being detained so long, their supply was almost exhausted. They had previously visited the island on several occasions, and made themselves at home with the people from the mainland who were temporarily resident upon it.

"The old bar at its best was never very safe for navigation, and this evening it was in its element, as with every storm it presented one boiling, seething mass of foam. The inhabitants of the island saw the frail small boat from the ship securely inside the bar, and prophesied some dire calamity should the captain and the two sailors venture to return to the ship that night. But the captain and his companions, having secured sufficient provisions, decided (as far as I can remember the story), even in spite of the entreaties of those on shore, to return to the ship. The storm was increasing, and what with their scanty knowledge of the intricacies of the channel, and the darkness of the night, certain it was the next morning their craft was found washed ashore on the island, and the body of the captain was discovered by the first man who made the round of the shore looking for logs of timber, or other useful articles washed ashore from wrecks. The bodies of the two sailors were never recovered, and word was sent immediately to the captain's wife in Derry, who came in a few days and gave directions for the disposal of her husband's corpse.

"The island was only temporarily inhabited by a few people who had cattle and horses grazing there for some weeks in the year, and after this catastrophe they felt peculiarly lonely, and sought refuge from their thoughts by all spending the evening together in one house. This particular evening they were all seated round the fire having a chat, when they heard steps approaching the door. Though the approach was fine, soft sand, yet the steps were audible as if coming on hard ground. They knew there was no one on the island save the few who were sitting quietly round the fire, and so in eager expectation they faced round to the door. What was their amazement when the door opened, and a tall, broad-shouldered man appeared and filled the whole doorway—and that man the captain who had been buried several days previously. He wore the identical suit in which he had often visited the island and even the "cheese-cutter" cap, so common a feature of sea-faring men's apparel, was not wanting. All were struck dumb with terror, and a woman who sat in a corner opposite the door, exclaimed in Irish in a low voice to my father:

"'O God! Patrick, there's the captain.'

"My father, recovering from the first shock, when he saw feminine courage finding expression in words, said in Irish to the apparition:

"'Come in!'

"They were so certain of the appearance that they addressed him in his own language, as they invariably talked Irish in the district in those days. But no sooner had he uttered the invitation than the figure, without the least word or sign, moved back, and disappeared from their view. They rushed out, but could discover no sign of any living person within the confines of the island. Such is the true account of an accident, by which three men lost their lives, and the ghostly sequel, in which one of them appeared to the eyes of four people, two of whom are yet alive, and can vouch for the accuracy of this narrative."

Group III

We now come to the third group of this chapter, in which we shall relate two first-hand experiences of tragedies being actually witnessed some time before they happened, as well as a reliable second-hand story of an apparition being seen two days before the death occurred. The first of these is sent by a lady, the percipient, who desires that her name be suppressed; with it was enclosed a letter from a gentleman who stated that he could testify to the truth of the following facts:

"The morning of May 18, 1902, was one of the worst that ever dawned in Killarney. All through the day a fierce nor'-wester raged, and huge white-crested waves, known locally as 'The O'Donoghue's white horses,' beat on the shores of Lough Leane. Then followed hail-showers such as I have never seen before or since. Hailstones quite as large as small marbles fell with such rapidity, and seemed so hard that the glass in the windows of the room in which I stood appeared to be about to break into fragments every moment. I remained at the window, gazing out on the turbulent waters of the lake. Sometimes a regular fog appeared, caused by the terrible downpour of rain and the fury of the gale.

"During an occasional lull I could see the islands plainly looming in the distance. In one of these clear intervals, the time being about 12.30 P.M., five friends of mine were reading in the room in which I stood. 'Quick! quick!' I cried. 'Is that a boat turned over?' My friends all ran to the windows, but could see nothing. I persisted, however, and said, 'It is on its side, with the keel turned towards us, and it is empty.' Still none of my friends could see anything. I then ran out, and got one of the men-servants to go down to a gate, about one hundred yards nearer the lake than where I stood. He had a powerful telescope, and remained with great difficulty in the teeth of the storm with his glass for several minutes, but could see nothing. When he returned another man took his place, but he also failed to see anything.

"I seemed so distressed that those around me kept going backwards and forwards to the windows, and then asked me what was the size of the boat I had seen. I gave them the exact size, measuring by landmarks. They then assured me that I must be absolutely wrong, as it was on rare occasions that a 'party' boat, such as the one I described, could venture on the lakes on such a day. Therefore there were seven persons who thought I was wrong in what I had seen. I still contended that I saw the boat, the length of which I described, as plainly as possible.

"The day wore on, and evening came. The incident was apparently more or less forgotten by all but me, until at 8 A.M. on the following morning, when the maid brought up tea, her first words were, 'Ah, miss, is it not terrible about the accident!' Naturally I said, 'What accident, Mary?' She replied, 'There were thirteen people drowned yesterday evening out of a four-oared boat.' That proved that the boat I had seen at 12.30 P.M. was a vision foreshadowing the wreck of the boat off Darby's Garden at 5.30 P.M. The position, shape, and size of the boat seen by me were identical with the one that was lost on the evening of May 18, 1902."

The second story relates how a lady witnessed a vision (shall we call it) of a suicide a week before the terrible deed was committed. This incident surely makes it clear that such cannot be looked upon as special interventions of Providence, for if the lady had recognised the man, she might have prevented his rash act. Mrs. MacAlpine says: "In June 1889, I drove to Castleblaney, in Co. Monaghan, to meet my sister: I expected her at three o'clock, but as she did not come by that train, I put up the horse and went for a walk in the demesne. At length becoming tired, I sat down on a rock by the edge of a lake. My attention was quite taken up with the beauty of the scene before me, as it was a glorious summer's day. Presently I felt a cold chill creep through me, and a curious stiffness came over my limbs, as if I could not move, though wishing to do so. I felt frightened, yet chained to the spot, and as if impelled to stare at the water straight before me. Gradually a black cloud seemed to rise, and in the midst of it I saw a

95

tall man, in a tweed suit, jump into the water, and sink. In a moment the darkness was gone, and I again became sensible of the heat and sunshine, but I was awed, and felt eerie. This happened about June 25, and on July 3 a Mr. ———, a bank clerk, committed suicide by drowning himself in the lake."

The following incident occurred in the United States, but, as it is closely connected with this country, it will not seem out of place to insert it here. It is sent by Mr. Richard Hogan as the personal experience of his sister, Mrs. Mary Murnane, and is given in her own words.

"On the 4th of August 1886, at 10.30 o'clock in the morning, I left my own house, 21 Montrose St., Philadelphia, to do some shopping. I had not proceeded more than fifty yards when on turning the corner of the street I observed my aunt approaching me within five or six yards. I was greatly astonished, for the last letter I had from home (Limerick) stated that she was dying of consumption, but the thought occurred to me that she might have recovered somewhat, and come out to Philadelphia. This opinion was quickly changed as we approached each other, for our eyes met, and she had the colour of one who had risen from the grave. I seemed to feel my hair stand on end, for just as we were about to pass each other she turned her face towards me, and I gasped, 'My God, she is dead, and is going to speak to me!' but no word was spoken, and she passed on. After proceeding a short distance I looked back, and she continued on to Washington Avenue, where she disappeared from me. There was no other person near at the time, and being so close, I was well able to note what she wore. She held a sunshade over her head, and the clothes, hat, &c., were those I knew so well before I left Ireland. I wrote home telling what I had seen, and asking if she was dead. I received a reply saying she was not dead at the date I saw her, but had been asking if a letter had come from me for some days before her death. It was just two days before she actually died that I had seen her."

CHAPTER VII

Banshees, and Other Death-Warnings

Of all Irish ghosts, fairies, or bogles, the Banshee (sometimes called locally the "Boheentha" or "Bankeentha") is the best known to the general public: indeed, cross-Channel visitors would class her with pigs, potatoes, and other fauna and flora of Ireland, and would expect her to make manifest her presence to them as being one of the sights of the country. She is a spirit with a lengthy pedigree—how lengthy no man can say, as its roots go back into the dim, mysterious past. The most famous Banshee of ancient times was that attached to the kingly house of O'Brien, Aibhill, who haunted the rock of Craglea above Killaloe, near the old palace of Kincora. In A.D. 1014 was fought the battle of Clontarf, from which the aged king, Brian Boru, knew that he would never come away alive, for the previous night Aibhill had appeared to him to tell him of his impending fate. The Banshee's method of foretelling death in olden times differed from that adopted by her at the present day: now she wails and wrings her hands, as a general rule, but in the old Irish tales she is to be found washing human heads and limbs, or blood-stained clothes, till the water is all dyed with human blood—this would take place before a battle. So it would seem that in the course of centuries her attributes and characteristics have changed somewhat.

Very different descriptions are given of her personal appearance. Sometimes she is young and beautiful, sometimes old and of a fearsome appearance. One writer describes her as "a tall, thin woman with uncovered head, and long hair that floated round her shoulders, attired in something which seemed either a loose white cloak, or a sheet thrown hastily around her, uttering piercing cries." Another person, a coachman, saw her one evening sitting on a stile in the yard; she seemed to be a very small woman, with blue eyes, long light hair, and wearing a red cloak. Other descriptions will be found in this chapter. By the way, it does not seem to be true that the Banshee exclusively follows families of Irish descent, for the last incident had reference to the death of a member of a Co. Galway family English by name and origin.

One of the oldest and best-known Banshee stories is that related in the *Memoirs* of Lady Fanshaw (Scott's *Lady of the Lake*, notes to Canto III, edition of 1811). In 1642 her husband, Sir Richard, and she chanced to visit a friend, the head of an Irish sept, who resided in his ancient baronial castle, surrounded with a moat. At midnight she was awakened by a ghastly and supernatural scream, and looking out of bed, beheld in the moonlight a female face and part of the form hovering at the window. The distance from the ground, as well as the circumstance of the moat, excluded the possibility that what she beheld was of this world. The face was that of a young and rather handsome woman, but pale, and the hair, which was reddish, was loose and dishevelled. The dress, which Lady Fanshaw's terror did not prevent her remarking accurately, was that of the ancient Irish. This apparition continued to exhibit itself for some time, and then vanished with two shrieks similar to that which had first excited Lady Fanshaw's attention. In the morning, with infinite terror, she communicated to her host what she had witnessed, and found him prepared not only to credit, but to account for the superstition. "A near relation of my family," said he, "expired last night in this castle. We disguised our certain expectation of the event from you, lest it should throw a cloud over the cheerful

98

reception which was your due. Now, before such an event happens in this family or castle, the female spectre whom you have seen is always visible. She is believed to be the spirit of a woman of inferior rank, whom one of my ancestors degraded himself by marrying, and whom afterwards, to expiate the dishonour done to his family, he caused to be drowned in the moat." In strictness this woman could hardly be termed a Banshee. The motive for the haunting is akin to that in the tale of the Scotch "Drummer of Cortachy," where the spirit of the murdered man haunts the family out of revenge, and appears before a death.

Mr. T. J. Westropp, M.A., has furnished the following story: "My maternal grandmother heard the following tradition from her mother, one of the Miss Ross-Lewins, who witnessed the occurrence. Their father, Mr. Harrison Ross-Lewin, was away in Dublin on law business, and in his absence the young people went off to spend the evening with a friend who lived some miles away. The night was fine and lightsome as they were returning, save at one point where the road ran between trees or high hedges not far to the west of the old church of Kilchrist. The latter, like many similar ruins, was a simple oblong building, with long side-walls and high gables, and at that time it and its graveyard were unenclosed, and lay in the open fields. As the party passed down the long dark lane they suddenly heard in the distance loud keening and clapping of hands, as the country-people were accustomed to do when lamenting the dead. The Ross-Lewins hurried on, and came in sight of the church, on the side wall of which a little gray-haired old woman, clad in a dark cloak, was running to and fro, chanting and wailing, and throwing up her arms. The girls were very frightened, but the young men ran forward and surrounded the ruin, and two of them went into the church, the apparition vanishing from the wall as they did so. They searched every nook, and found no one, nor did anyone pass out. All were now well scared, and got home as fast as possible. On reaching

99

their home their mother opened the door, and at once told them that she was in terror about their father, for, as she sat looking out the window in the moonlight, a huge raven with fiery eyes lit on the sill, and tapped three times on the glass. They told her their story, which only added to their anxiety, and as they stood talking, taps came to the nearest window, and they saw the bird again. A few days later news reached them that Mr. Ross-Lewin had died suddenly in Dublin. This occurred about 1776."

Mr. Westropp also writes that the sister of a former Roman Catholic Bishop told his sisters that when she was a little girl she went out one evening with some other children for a walk. Going down the road, they passed the gate of the principal demesne near the town. There was a rock, or large stone, beside the road, on which they saw something. Going nearer, they perceived it to be a little dark, old woman, who began crying and clapping her hands. Some of them attempted to speak to her, but got frightened, and all finally ran home as quickly as they could. Next day the news came that the gentleman, near whose gate the Banshee had cried, was dead, and it was found on inquiry that he had died at the very hour at which the children had seen the spectre.

A lady who is a relation of one of the compilers, and a member of a Co. Cork family of English descent, sends the two following experiences of a Banshee in her family. "My mother, when a young girl, was standing looking out of the window in their house at Blackrock, near Cork. She suddenly saw a white figure standing on a bridge which was easily visible from the house. The figure waved her arms towards the house, and my mother heard the bitter wailing of the Banshee. It lasted some seconds, and then the figure disappeared. Next morning my grandfather was walking as usual into the city of Cork. He accidentally fell, hit his head against the curbstone, and never recovered consciousness.

"In March 1900, my mother was very ill, and one evening the nurse and I were with her arranging her bed. We suddenly heard the most extraordinary wailing, which seemed to come in waves round and under her bed. We naturally looked everywhere to try and find the cause, but in vain. The nurse and I looked at one another, but made no remark, as my mother did not seem to hear it. My sister was downstairs sitting with my father. She heard it, and thought some terrible thing had happened to her little boy, who was in bed upstairs. She rushed up, and found him sleeping quietly. My father did not hear it. In the house next door they heard it, and ran downstairs, thinking something had happened to the servant; but the latter at once said to them, 'Did you hear the Banshee? Mrs. P— must be dying.'"

A few years ago (*i.e.* before 1894) a curious incident occurred in a public school in connection with the belief in the Banshee. One of the boys, happening to become ill, was at once placed in a room by himself, where he used to sit all day. On one occasion, as he was being visited by the doctor, he suddenly started up from his seat, and affirmed that he heard somebody crying. The doctor, of course, who could hear or see nothing, came to the conclusion that the illness had slightly affected his brain. However, the boy, who appeared quite sensible, still persisted that he heard someone crying, and furthermore said, "It is the Banshee, as I have heard it before." The following morning the head-master received a telegram saying that the boy's brother had been accidentally shot dead.[1]

That the Banshee is not confined within the geographical limits of Ireland, but that she can follow the fortunes of a family

---

[1] A. G. Bradley, *Notes on some Irish Superstitions*, p. 9.

abroad, and there foretell their death, is clearly shown by the following story. A party of visitors were gathered together on the deck of a private yacht on one of the Italian lakes, and during a lull in the conversation one of them, a Colonel, said to the owner, "Count, who's that queer-looking woman you have on board?" The Count replied that there was nobody except the ladies present, and the stewardess, but the speaker protested that he was correct, and suddenly, with a scream of horror, he placed his hands before his eyes, and exclaimed, "Oh, my God, what a face!" For some time he was overcome with terror, and at length reluctantly looked up, and cried:

"Thank Heavens, it's gone!"

"What was it?" asked the Count.

"Nothing human," replied the Colonel—"nothing belonging to this world. It was a woman of no earthly type, with a queer-shaped, gleaming face, a mass of red hair, and eyes that would have been beautiful but for their expression, which was hellish. She had on a green hood, after the fashion of an Irish peasant."

An American lady present suggested that the description tallied with that of the Banshee, upon which the Count said:

"I am an O'Neill—at least I am descended from one. My family name is, as you know, Neilsini, which, little more than a century ago, was O'Neill. My great-grandfather served in the Irish Brigade, and on its dissolution at the time of the French Revolution had the good fortune to escape the general massacre of officers, and in company with an O'Brien and a Maguire fled across the frontier and settled in Italy. On his death his son, who had been born in Italy, and was far more Italian than Irish, changed his name to Neilsini, by which name the family has been known ever since. But for all that we are Irish."

"The Banshee was yours, then!" ejaculated the Colonel. "What exactly does it mean?"

"It means," the Count replied solemnly, "the death of some one very nearly associated with me. Pray Heaven it is not my wife or daughter."

On that score, however, his anxiety was speedily removed, for within two hours he was seized with a violent attack of angina pectoris, and died before morning.[1]

Mr. Elliott O'Donnell, to whose article on "Banshees" we are indebted for the above, adds: "The Banshee never manifests itself to the person whose death it is prognosticating. Other people may see or hear it, but the fated one never, so that when everyone present is aware of it but one, the fate of that one may be regarded as pretty well certain."

We must now pass on from the subject of Banshees to the kindred one of "Headless Coaches," the belief in which is widespread through the country. Apparently these dread vehicles must be distinguished from the phantom coaches, of which numerous circumstantial tales are also told. The first are harbingers of death, and in this connection are very often attached to certain families; the latter appear to be spectral phenomena pure and simple, whose appearance does not necessarily portend evil or death.

"At a house in Co. Limerick," writes Mr. T. J. Westropp, "occurred the remarkably-attested apparition of the headless coach in June 1806, when Mr. Ralph Westropp, my great-grandfather, lay dying. The story was told by his sons, John, William, and Ralph, to their respective children, who told it to me. They had sent for the doctor, and were awaiting his arrival in the dusk. As they sat on the steps they suddenly heard a heavy rumbling, and saw a huge dark coach drive into the paved court before the door. One of them went down to meet the doctor, but the coach swept past him, and drove down the avenue, which went straight between the fences and hedges to a gate. Two of the young men ran after the coach, which they could hear rumbling before them,

---

[1] *Occult Review* for September, 1913.

103

and suddenly came full tilt against the avenue gate. The noise had stopped, and they were surprised at not finding the carriage. The gate proved to be locked, and when they at last awoke the lodge-keeper, he showed them the keys under his pillow; the doctor arrived a little later, but could do nothing, and the sick man died a few hours afterwards."

Two other good stories come from Co. Clare. One night in April 1821, two servants were sitting up to receive a son of the family, Cornelius O'Callaghan, who had travelled in vain for his health, and was returning home. One of them, Halloran, said that the heavy rumble of a coach roused them. The other servant, Burke, stood on the top of the long flight of steps with a lamp, and sent Halloran down to open the carriage door. He reached out his hand to do so, saw a skeleton looking out, gave one yell, and fell in a heap. When the badly-scared Burke picked himself up there was no sign or sound of any coach. A little later the invalid arrived, so exhausted that he died suddenly in the early morning.

On the night of December 11, 1876, a servant of the MacNamaras was going his rounds at Ennistymon, a beautiful spot in a wooded glen, with a broad stream falling in a series of cascades. In the dark he heard the rumbling of wheels on the back avenue, and, knowing from the hour and place that no mortal vehicle could be coming, concluded that it was the death coach, and ran on, opening the gates before it. He had just time to open the third gate, and throw himself on his face beside it, when he heard a coach go clanking past. On the following day Admiral Sir Burton MacNamara died in London.

Mr. Westropp informs us that at sight or sound of this coach all gates should be thrown open, and then it will not stop at the house to call for a member of the family, but will only foretell the death of some relative at a distance. We hope our readers will carefully bear in mind this simple method of averting fate.

We may conclude this chapter with some account of strange and varied death-warnings, which are attached to certain families and foretell the coming of the King of Terrors.

In a Co. Wicklow family a death is preceded by the appearance of a spectre; the doors of the sitting-room open and a lady dressed in white satin walks across the room and hall. Before any member of a certain Queen's Co. family died a looking-glass was broken; while in a branch of that family the portent was the opening and shutting of the avenue gate. In another Queen's Co. family approaching death was heralded by the cry of the cuckoo, no matter at what season of the year it might occur. A Mrs. F— and her son lived near Clonaslee. One day, in mid-winter, their servant heard a cuckoo; they went out for a drive, the trap jolted over a stone, throwing Mrs. F— out, and breaking her neck. The ringing of all the house-bells is another portent which seems to be attached to several families. In another the æolian harp is heard at or before death; an account of this was given to the present writer by a clergyman, who declares that he heard it in the middle of the night when one of his relatives passed away. A death-warning in the shape of a white owl follows the Westropp family. This last appeared, it is said, before a death in 1909, but, as Mr. T. J. Westropp remarks, it would be more convincing if it appeared at places where the white owl does *not* nest and fly out every night. No doubt this list might be drawn out to much greater length.

A lady correspondent states that her cousin, a Sir Patrick Dun's nurse, was attending a case in the town of Wicklow. Her patient was a middle-aged woman, the wife of a well-to-do shopkeeper. One evening the nurse was at her tea in the dining-room beneath the sick-room, when suddenly she heard a tremendous crash overhead. Fearing her patient had fallen out of bed, she hurried upstairs, to find her dozing quietly, and there was not the least sign of any disturbance. A member of the family, to whom she related this, told her calmly that that noise was always heard in their house before the death of any of them, and that it was a sure sign that the invalid would not recover. Contrary to the nurse's expectations, she died the following day.

Knocking on the door is another species of death-warning. The Rev. D. B. Knox writes: "On the evening before the wife of a clerical friend of mine died, the knocker of the hall-door was loudly rapped. All in the room heard it. The door was opened, but there was no one there. Again the knocker was heard, but no one was to be seen when the door was again opened. A young man, brother of the dying woman, went into the drawing-room, and looked through one of the drawing-room windows. The full light of the moon fell on the door, and as he looked the knocker was again lifted and loudly rapped."

The following portent occurs in a Co. Cork family. At one time the lady of the house lay ill, and her two daughters were aroused one night by screams proceeding from their mother's room. They rushed in, and found her sitting up in bed, staring at some object unseen to them, but which, from the motion of her eyes, appeared to be moving across the floor. When she became calm she told them, what they had not known before, that members of the family were sometimes warned of the death, or approaching death, of some other member by the appearance of a ball of fire, which would pass slowly through the room; this phenomenon she had just witnessed. A day or two afterwards the mother heard of the death of her brother, who lived in the Colonies.

A strange appearance, known as the "Scanlan Lights," is connected with the family of Scanlan of Ballyknockane, Co. Limerick, and is seen frequently at the death of a member. The traditional origin of the lights is connected with a well-known Irish legend, which we give here briefly. Scanlan Mor (died A.D. 640), King of Ossory, from whom the family claim descent, was suspected of disaffection by Aedh mac Ainmire, Ard-Righ of Ireland, who cast him into prison, and loaded him with fetters. When St. Columcille attended the Synod of Drom Ceat, he besought Aedh to free his captive, but the Ard-Righ churlishly refused; whereupon Columcille declared that he should be freed, and that that very night he should unloose his (the Saint's) brogues. Columcille went away, and that night a bright pillar of fire appeared in the air, and hung over the house where Scanlan was imprisoned. A beam of light darted into the room where he lay, and a voice called to him, bidding him rise, and shake off his fetters. In amazement he did so, and was led out past his guards by an angel. He made his way to Columcille, with whom he was to continue that night, and as the Saint stooped down to unloose his brogues Scanlan anticipated him, as he had prophesied.

Such appears to be the traditional origin of the "Scanlan lights." Our correspondent adds: "These are always seen at the demise of a member of the family. We have ascertained that by the present head of the family (Scanlan of Ballyknockane) they were seen, first, as a pillar of fire with radiated crown at the top; and secondly, inside the house, by the room being lighted up brightly in the night. By other members of the family now living these lights have been seen in the shape of balls of fire of various sizes." The above was copied from a private manuscript written some few years ago. Our correspondent further states: "I also have met with four persons in this county [Limerick] who have seen the lights on Knockfierna near Ballyknockane before the death of a Scanlan, one of the four being the late head of the family and owner, William Scanlan, J.P., who saw the flames on the hill-side on the day of his aunt's death some years ago. The last occasion was as late as 1913, on the eve of the death of a Scanlan related to the present owner of Ballyknockane."

In front of the residence of the G— family in Co. Galway there is, or formerly was, a round ring of grass surrounded by a low evergreen hedge. The lady who related this story to our informant stated that one evening dinner was kept waiting for Mr. G—, who was absent in town on some business. She went out on the hall-door steps in order to see if the familiar trot of the carriage horses could be heard coming down the road. It was a bright moonlight night, and as she stood there she heard a child crying with a peculiar whining cry, and distinctly saw a small childlike figure running round and round the grass ring inside the evergreen hedge, and casting a shadow in the moonlight. Going into the house she casually mentioned this as a peculiar circumstance to Mrs. G—, upon which, to her great surprise, that lady nearly fainted, and got into a terrible state of nervousness. Recovering a little, she told her that this crying and figure were always heard and seen whenever any member met with an accident, or before a death. A messenger was immediately sent to meet Mr. G—, who was found lying senseless on the road, as the horses had taken fright and bolted, flinging him out, and breaking the carriage-pole.

But of all the death-warnings in connection with Irish families surely the strangest is the Gormanstown foxes. The crest of that noble family is a running fox, while the same animal also forms one of the supporters of the coat-of-arms. The story is, that when the head of the house is dying the foxes—not spectral foxes, but creatures of flesh and blood—leave the coverts and congregate at Gormanstown Castle.

Let us see what proof there is of this. When Jenico, the 12th Viscount, was dying in 1860, foxes were seen about the house and moving towards the house for some days previously. Just before his death three foxes were playing about and making a noise close to the house, and just in front of the "cloisters," which are yew-trees planted and trained in that shape. The Hon. Mrs. Farrell states as regards the same that the foxes came in pairs into the demesne, and sat under the Viscount's bedroom window, and barked and howled all night. Next morning they were to be found crouching about in the grass in front and around the house. They walked through the poultry and never touched them. After the funeral they disappeared.

At the death of Edward, the 13th Viscount, in 1876, the foxes were also there. He had been rather better one day, but the foxes appeared, barking under the window, and he died that night contrary to expectation.

On October 28, 1907, Jenico, the 14th Viscount, died in Dublin. About 8 o'clock that night the coachman and gardener saw two foxes near the chapel (close to the house), five or six more round the front of the house, and several crying in the "cloisters." Two days later the Hon. Richard Preston, R.F.A., was watching by his father's body in the above chapel. About 3 A.M. he became conscious of a slight noise, which seemed to be that of a number of people walking stealthily around the chapel on the gravel walk. He went to the side door, listened, and heard outside a continuous and insistent snuffling or sniffing noise, accompanied by whimperings and scratchings at the door. On opening it he saw a full-grown fox sitting on the path within four feet of him. Just in the shadow was another, while he could hear several more moving close by in the darkness. He then went to the end door, opposite the altar, and on opening it saw two more foxes, one so close that he could have touched it with his foot. On shutting the door the noise continued till 5 A.M., when it suddenly ceased.[1]

---

[1] *New Ireland Review* for April 1908.

CHAPTER VIII

Miscellaneous Supernormal Experiences

THE MATTER IN this chapter does not seem, strictly speaking, to come under the head of any of the preceding ones: it contains no account of houses or places permanently haunted, or of warnings of impending death. Rather we have gathered up in it a number of tales relative to the appearance of the "wraiths" of living men, or accounts of visions, strange apparitions, or extraordinary experiences; some few of these have a purpose, while the majority are strangely aimless and purposeless—something is seen or heard, that is all, and no results, good or bad, follow.

We commence with one which, however, certainly indicates a purpose which was fulfilled. It is the experience of Mrs. Seymour, wife to one of the compilers. When she was a little girl she resided in Dublin; amongst the members of the family was her paternal grandmother. This old lady was not as kind as she might have been to her grand-daughter, and consequently the latter was somewhat afraid of her. In process of time the grandmother died. Mrs. Seymour, who was then about eight years of age, had to pass the door of the room where the death occurred in order to reach her own bedroom, which was a flight higher up. Past this door the child used to fly in terror with all possible speed. On one occasion, however, as she was preparing to make the usual rush past, she distinctly felt a hand placed on her shoulder, and became conscious of a voice saying, "Don't be afraid, Mary!"

From that day on the child never had the least feeling of fear, and always walked quietly past the door.

The Rev. D. B. Knox sends a curious personal experience, which was shared by him with three other people. He writes as follows: "Not very long ago my wife and I were preparing to retire for the night. A niece, who was in the house, was in her bedroom and the door was open. The maid had just gone to her room. All four of us distinctly heard the heavy step of a man walking along the corridor, apparently in the direction of the bathroom. We searched the whole house immediately, but no one was discovered. Nothing untoward happened except the death of the maid's mother about a fortnight later. It was a detached house, so that the noise could not have been made by the neighbours."

In the following tale the "double" or "wraith" of a living man was seen by three different people, one of whom, our correspondent, saw it through a telescope. She writes: "In May 1883 the parish of A— was vacant, so Mr. D—, the Diocesan Curate, used to come out to take service on Sundays. One day there were two funerals to be taken, the one at a graveyard some distance off, the other at A— churchyard. My brother was at both, the far-off one being taken the first. The house we then lived in looked down towards A— churchyard, which was about a quarter of a mile away. From an upper window my sister and I saw *two* surpliced figures going out to meet the coffin, and said, 'Why, there are two clergy!' having supposed that there would be only Mr. D—. I, being short-sighted, used a telescope, and saw the two surplices showing between the people. But when my brother returned he said, 'A strange thing has happened. Mr. D— and Mr. W— (curate of a neighbouring parish) took the far-off funeral. I saw them both again at A—, but when I went into the vestry I only saw Mr. W—. I asked where Mr. D— was, and he replied that he had left immediately after the first funeral, as he had to go to Kilkenny, and that he (Mr. W—) had come on *alone* to take the funeral at A—.'"

Here is a curious tale from the city of Limerick of a lady's "double" being seen, with no consequent results. It is sent by Mr. Richard Hogan as the personal experience of his sister, Mrs. Mary Murnane. On Saturday, October 25, 1913, at half-past four o'clock in the afternoon, Mr. Hogan left the house in order to purchase some cigarettes. A quarter of an hour afterwards Mrs. Murnane went down the town to do some business. As she was walking down George Street she saw a group of four persons standing on the pavement engaged in conversation. They were: her brother, a Mr. O'S—, and two ladies, a Miss P. O'D—, and her sister, Miss M. O'D—. She recognised the latter, as her face was partly turned towards her, and noted that she was dressed in a knitted coat, and light blue hat, while in her left hand she held a bag or purse; the other lady's back was turned towards her. As Mrs. Murnane was in a hurry to get her business done she determined to pass them by without being noticed, but a number of people coming in the opposite direction blocked the way, and compelled her to walk quite close to the group of four; but they were so intent on listening to what one lady was saying that they took no notice of her. The speaker appeared to be Miss M. O'D—, and, though Mrs. Murnane did not actually hear her *speak* as she passed her, yet from their attitudes the other three seemed to be listening to what she was saying, and she heard her *laugh* when right behind her—not the laugh of her sister P.— and the laugh was repeated after she had left the group a little behind.

So far there is nothing out of the common. When Mrs. Murnane returned to her house about an hour later she found her brother Richard there before her. She casually mentioned to him how she had passed him and his three companions on the pavement. To which he replied that she was quite correct except in one point, namely that there were only *three* in the group, as M. O'D—*was not present*, as she had not come to Limerick at all that day. She then described to him the exact position each one of the four occupied, and the clothes worn by them; to all of which facts he assented, except as to the presence of Miss M. O'D—. Mrs. Murnane adds, "That is all I can say in the matter, but most certainly the fourth person was in the group, as I both saw and heard her. She wore the same clothes I had seen on her previously, with the exception of the hat; but the following Saturday she had on the same coloured hat I had seen on her the previous Saturday. When I told her about it she was as much mystified as I was and am. My brother stated that there was no laugh from any of the three present."

Mrs. G. Kelly sends an experience of a "wraith," which seems in some mysterious way to have been conjured up in her mind by the description she had heard, and then externalised. She writes: "About four years ago a musical friend of ours was staying in the house. He and my husband were playing and singing Dvorak's *Spectre's Bride,* a work which he had studied with the composer himself. This music appealed very much to both, and they were excited and enthusiastic over it. Our friend was giving many personal reminiscences of Dvorak, and his method of explaining the way he wanted his work done. I was sitting by, an interested listener, for some time. On getting up at last, and going into the drawing-room, I was startled and somewhat frightened to find a man standing there in a shadowy part of the room. I saw him distinctly, and could describe his appearance accurately. I called out, and the two men ran in, but as the apparition only lasted for a second, they were too late. I described the man whom I had seen, whereupon our friend exclaimed, 'Why, that was Dvorak himself!' At that time I had never seen a picture of Dvorak, but when our friend returned to London he

114

sent me one which I recognised as the likeness of the man whom I had seen in our drawing-room."

A curious vision, a case of second sight, in which a quite unimportant event, previously unknown, was revealed, is sent by the percipient, who is a lady well known to both the compilers, and a life-long friend of one of them. She says: "Last summer I sent a cow to the fair of Limerick, a distance of about thirteen miles, and the men who took her there the day before the fair left her in a paddock for the night close to Limerick city. I awoke up very early next morning, and was fully awake when I saw (not with my ordinary eyesight, but apparently *inside* my head) a light, an intensely brilliant light, and in it I saw the back gate being opened by a red-haired woman and the cow I had supposed in the fair walking through the gate. I then knew that the cow must be home, and going to the yard later on I was met by the wife of the man who was in charge in a great state of excitement. 'Oh law! Miss,' she exclaimed, 'you'll be mad! Didn't Julia [a red-haired woman] find the cow outside the lodge gate as she was going out at 4 o'clock to the milking!' That's my tale—perfectly true, and I would give a good deal to be able to control that light, and see more if I could."

Another curious vision was seen by a lady who is also a friend of both the compilers. One night she was kneeling at her bedside saying her prayers (hers was the only bed in the room), when suddenly she felt a distinct touch on her shoulder. She turned round in the direction of the touch and saw at the end of the room a bed, with a pale, indistinguishable figure laid therein, and what appeared to be a clergyman standing over it. About a week later she fell into a long and dangerous illness.

An account of a dream which implied an extraordinary coincidence, if coincidence it be and nothing more, was sent as follows by a correspondent, who requested that no names be published. "That which I am about to relate has a peculiar interest for me, inasmuch as the central figure in it was my own grand-aunt, and moreover the principal witness (if I may use such a term) was my father. At the period during which this strange incident occurred my father was living with his aunt and some other relatives.

"One morning at the breakfast-table, my grand-aunt announced that she had had a most peculiar dream during the previous night. My father, who was always very interested in that kind of thing, took down in his notebook all the particulars concerning it. They were as follows.

"My grand-aunt dreamt that she was in a cemetery, which she recognised as Glasnevin, and as she gazed at the memorials of the dead which lay so thick around, one stood out most conspicuously, and caught her eye, for she saw clearly cut on the cold white stone *an inscription bearing her own name:*

CLARE S · D—
Died 14th of March, 1873
Dearly loved and ever mourned.
R.I.P.

while, to add to the peculiarity of it, the date on the stone as given above was, from the day of her dream, exactly a year in advance.

"My grand-aunt was not very nervous, and soon the dream faded from her mind. Months rolled by, and one morning at breakfast it was noticed that my grand-aunt had not appeared, but as she was a very religious woman it was thought that she had gone out to church. However, as she did not appear my father sent someone to her room to see if she were there, and as no answer was given to repeated knocking the door was opened, and my grand-aunt was found kneeling at her bedside, dead. The day of her death was March 14, 1873, corresponding exactly with the date seen in her dream a twelvemonth before. My grand-aunt was buried in Glasnevin, and on her tombstone (a white marble slab) was placed the inscription which she had read in her dream." Our correspondent sent us a photograph of the stone and its inscription.

The present Archdeacon of Limerick, Ven. J. A. Haydn, LL.D., sends the following experience: "In the year 1870 I was rector of the little rural parish of Chapel Russell. One autumn day the rain fell with a quiet, steady, and hopeless persistence from morning to night. Wearied at length from the gloom, and tired of reading and writing, I determined to walk to the church about half a mile away, and pass a half-hour playing the harmonium, returning for the lamp-light and tea.

"I wrapped up, put the key of the church in my pocket, and started. Arriving at the church, I walked up the straight avenue, bordered with graves and tombs on either side, while the soft, steady rain quietly pattered on the trees. When I reached the church door, before putting the key in the lock, moved by some indefinable impulse, I stood on the doorstep, turned round, and looked back upon the path I had just trodden. My amazement may be imagined when I saw, seated on a low, tabular tombstone close to the avenue, a lady with her back towards me. She was wearing a black velvet jacket or short cape, with a narrow border of vivid white: her head, and luxuriant jet-black hair, were surmounted by a hat of the shape and make that I think used to be called at that time a "turban"; it was also of black velvet, with a snow-white wing or feather at the right-hand side of it. It may be seen how deliberately and minutely I observed the appearance, when I can thus recall it after more than forty years.

"Actuated by a desire to attract the attention of the lady, and induce her to look towards me, I noisily inserted the key in the door, and suddenly opened it with a rusty crack. Turning round to see the effect of my policy—the lady was gone!—vanished! Not yet daunted, I hurried to the place, which was not ten paces away, and closely searched the stone and the space all round it, but utterly in vain; there were absolutely no traces of the late presence of a human being! I may add that nothing particular or remarkable followed the singular apparition, and that I never heard anything calculated to throw any light on the mystery."

Here is a story of a ghost who knew what it wanted—and got it! "In the part of Co. Wicklow from which my people come," writes a Miss D—, "there was a family who were not exactly related, but of course of the clan. Many years ago a young daughter, aged about twenty, died. Before her death she had directed her parents to bury her in a certain graveyard. But for some reason they did not do so, and from that hour she gave them no peace. She appeared to them at all hours, especially when they went to the well for water. So distracted were they, that at length they got permission to exhume the remains and have them reinterred in the desired graveyard. This they did by torchlight— a weird scene truly! I can vouch for the truth of this latter portion, at all events, as some of my own relatives were present."

Mr. T. J. Westropp contributes a tale of a ghost of an unusual type, *i.e.* one which actually did communicate matters of importance to his family. "A lady who related many ghost stories to me, also told me how, after her father's death, the family could not find some papers or receipts of value. One night she awoke, and heard a sound which she at once recognised as the footsteps of her father, who was lame. The door creaked, and she prayed that she might be able to see him. Her prayer was granted: she saw him distinctly holding a yellow parchment book tied with tape. 'F—, child,' said he, 'this is the book your mother is looking for. It is in the third drawer of the cabinet near the cross-door; tell your mother to be more careful in future about business papers.' Incontinent he vanished, and she at once awoke her mother, in whose room she was sleeping, who was very angry and ridiculed the story, but the girl's earnestness at length impressed her. She got up, went to the old cabinet, and at once found the missing book in the third drawer."

Here is another tale of an equally useful and obliging ghost. "A gentleman, a relative of my own," writes a lady, "often received warnings from his dead father of things that were about to happen. Besides the farm on which he lived, he had another some miles away which adjoined a large demesne. Once in a great storm a fir-tree was blown down in the demesne, and fell into his field. The woodranger came to him and told him he might as well cut up the tree, and take it away. Accordingly one day he set out for this purpose, taking with him two men and a cart. He got into the fields by a stile, while his men went on to a gate. As he approached a gap between two fields he saw, standing in it, his father as plainly as he ever saw him in life, and beckoning him back warningly. Unable to understand this, he still advanced, whereupon his father looked very angry, and his gestures became imperious. This induced him to turn away, so he sent his men home, and left the tree uncut. He subsequently discovered that a plot had been laid by the woodranger, who coveted his farm, and who hoped to have him dispossessed by accusing him of stealing the tree."

A clergyman in the diocese of Clogher gave a personal experience of table-turning to the present Dean of St. Patrick's, who kindly sent the same to the writer. He said: "When I was a young man, I met some friends one evening, and we decided to amuse ourselves with table-turning. The local dispensary was vacant at the time, so we said that if the table would work we should ask who would be appointed as medical officer. As we sat round it touching it with our hands it began to knock. We said:

"'Who are you?'

"The table spelt out the name of a Bishop of the Church of Ireland. We asked, thinking that the answer was absurd, as we knew him to be alive and well:

"'Are you dead?'

"The table answered 'Yes.'

"We laughed at this and asked:

"'Who will be appointed to the dispensary?'

"The table spelt out the name of a stranger, who was not one of the candidates, whereupon we left off, thinking that the whole thing was nonsense.

"The next morning I saw in the papers that the Bishop in question had died that afternoon about two hours before our meeting, and a few days afterwards I saw the name of the stranger as the new dispensary doctor. I got such a shock that I determined never to have anything to do with table-turning again."

The following extraordinary personal experience is sent by a lady, well known to the present writer, but who requests that all names be omitted. Whatever explanation we may give of it, the good faith of the tale is beyond doubt.

"Two or three months after my father-in-law's death my husband, myself, and three small sons lived in the west of Ireland. As my husband was a young barrister, he had to be absent from home a good deal. My three boys slept in my bedroom, the eldest being about four, the youngest some months. A fire was kept up every night, and with a young child to look after, I was naturally awake more than once during the night. For many nights I believed I distinctly saw my father-in-law sitting by the fireside. This happened, not once or twice, but many times. He was passionately fond of his eldest grandson, who lay sleeping calmly in his cot. Being so much alone probably made me restless and uneasy, though I never felt *afraid*. I mentioned this strange thing to a friend who had known and liked my father-in-law, and she advised me to 'have his soul laid,' as she termed

120

it. Though I was a Protestant and she was a Roman Catholic (as had also been my father-in-law), yet I fell in with her suggestion. She told me to give a coin to the next beggar that came to the house, telling him (or her) to pray for the rest of Mr. So-and-so's soul. A few days later a beggar-woman and her children came to the door, to whom I gave a coin and stated my desire. To my great surprise I learned from her manner that such requests were not unusual. Well, she went down on her knees on the steps, and prayed with apparent earnestness and devotion that his soul might find repose. Once again he appeared, and seemed to say to me, 'Why did you do that, E—? To come and sit here was the only comfort I had.' Never again did he appear, and strange to say, after a lapse of more than thirty years I have felt regret at my selfishness in interfering.

"After his death, as he lay in the house awaiting burial, and I was in a house some ten miles away, I thought that he came and told me that I would have a hard life, which turned out only too truly. I was then young, and full of life, with every hope of a prosperous future."

Of all the strange beliefs to be found in Ireland that in the Black Dog is the most widespread. There is hardly a parish in the country but could contribute some tale relative to this spectre, though the majority of these are short, and devoid of interest. There is said to be such a dog just outside the avenue gate of Donohill Rectory, but neither of the compilers have had the good luck to see it. It may be, as some hold, that this animal was originally a cloud or nature-myth; at all events, it has now descended to the level of an ordinary haunting. The most circumstantial story that we have met with relative to the Black Dog is that related as follows by a clergyman of the Church of Ireland, who requests us to refrain from publishing his name.

"In my childhood I lived in the country. My father, in addition to his professional duties, sometimes did a little farming in

121

an amateurish sort of way. He did not keep a regular staff of labourers, and consequently when anything extra had to be done, such as hay-cutting or harvesting, he used to employ day-labourers to help with the work. At such times I used to enjoy being in the fields with the men, listening to their conversation. On one occasion I heard a labourer remark that he had once seen the devil! Of course I was interested and asked him to give me his experience. He said he was walking along a certain road, and when he came to a point where there was an entrance to a private place (the spot was well known to me), he saw a black dog sitting on the roadside. At the time he paid no attention to it, thinking it was an ordinary retriever, but after he had passed on about two or three hundred yards he found the dog was beside him, and then he noticed that its eyes were blood-red. He stooped down, and picked up some stones in order to frighten it away, but though he threw the stones at it they did not injure it, nor indeed did they seem to have any effect. Suddenly, after a few moments, the dog vanished from his sight.

"Such was the labourer's tale. After some years, during which time I had forgotten altogether about the man's story, some friends of my own bought the place at the entrance to which the apparition had been seen. When my friends went to reside there I was a constant visitor at their house. Soon after their arrival they began to be troubled by the appearance of a black dog. Though I never saw it myself, it appeared to many members of the family. The avenue leading to the house was a long one, and it was customary for the dog to appear and accompany people for the greater portion of the way. Such an effect had this on my friends that they soon gave up the house, and went to live elsewhere. This was a curious corroboration of the labourer's tale."

As we have already stated in Chapter VII, a distinction must be drawn between the so-called *Headless* Coach, which portends death, and the *Phantom* Coach, which appears to be a harmless sort of vehicle. With regard to the latter we give two tales below, the first of which was sent by a lady whose father was a clergyman, and a gold medalist of Trinity College, Dublin.

"Some years ago my family lived in Co. Down. Our house was some way out of a fair-sized manufacturing town, and had a short avenue which ended in a gravel sweep in front of the hall door. One winter's evening, when my father was returning from a sick call, a carriage going at a sharp pace passed him on the avenue. He hurried on, thinking it was some particular friends, but when he reached the door no carriage was to be seen, so he concluded it must have gone round to the stables. The servant who answered his ring said that no visitors had been there, and he, feeling certain that the girl had made some mistake, or that some one else had answered the door, came into the drawing-room to make further inquiries. No visitors had come, however, though those sitting in the drawing-room had also heard the carriage drive up.

"My father was most positive as to what he had seen, viz. a closed carriage with lamps lit; and let me say at once that he was a clergyman who was known throughout the whole of the north of Ireland as a most level-headed man, and yet to the day of his death he would insist that he met that carriage on our avenue.

"One day in July one of our servants was given leave to go home for the day, but was told she must return by a certain train. For some reason she did not come by it, but by a much later one, and rushed into the kitchen in a most penitent frame of mind. 'I am so sorry to be late,' she told the cook, 'especially as there were visitors. I suppose they stayed to supper, as they were so late going away, for I met the carriage on the avenue.' The cook thereupon told her that no one had been at the house, and hinted that she must have seen the ghost-carriage, a statement that alarmed her very much, as the story was well known in the town, and car-drivers used to whip up their horses as they passed our gate, while pedestrians refused to go at all except in numbers. We have often *heard* the carriage, but these are the only two occasions on which I can positively assert that it was *seen*."

The following personal experience of the phantom coach was given to the present writer by Mr. Matthias Fitzgerald, coachman to Miss Cooke, of Cappagh House, Co. Limerick. He stated that one moonlight night he was driving along the road from Askeaton to Limerick when he heard coming up behind him the roll of wheels, the clatter of horses' hoofs, and the jingling of the bits. He drew over to his own side to let this carriage pass, but nothing passed. He then looked back, but could see nothing, the road was perfectly bare and empty, though the sounds were perfectly audible. This continued for about a quarter of an hour or so, until he came to a cross-road, down one arm of which he had to turn. As he turned off he heard the phantom carriage dash by rapidly along the straight road. He stated that other persons had had similar experiences on the same road.

CHAPTER IX

Legendary and Ancestral Ghosts

WHATEVER EXPLANATIONS MAY be given of the various stories told in our previous chapters, the facts as stated therein are in almost every case vouched for on reliable authority. We now turn to stories of a different kind, most of which have no evidence of any value in support of the *facts*, but which have been handed down from generation to generation, and deserve our respect, if only for their antiquity. We make no apology for giving them here, for, in addition to the interesting reading they provide, they also serve a useful purpose as a contrast to authenticated ghost stories. The student of folklore will find parallels to some of them in the tales of other nations.

Lord Walter Fitzgerald sends us the following: "Garrett oge" (or Gerald the younger) "Fitzgerald, 11th Earl of Kildare, died in London on the 16th November 1585; his body was brought back to Ireland and interred in St. Brigid's Cathedral, in Kildare. He was known as 'the Wizard Earl' on account of his practising the black art, whereby he was enabled to transform himself into other shapes, either bird or beast according to his choice; so notorious was his supernatural power that he became the terror of the countryside.

"His wife, the Countess, had long wished to see some proof of his skill, and had frequently begged him to transform himself before her, but he had steadily refused to do so, as he said if he did and she became afraid, he would be taken from her, and she would never see him again. Still she persisted, and at last he said he would do as she wished on condition that she should first of all undergo three trials to test her courage; to this she willingly agreed. In the first trial the river Greese, which flows past the castle walls, at a sign from the Earl overflowed its banks and flooded the banqueting hall in which the Earl and Countess were sitting. She showed no sign of fear, and at the Earl's command the river receded to its normal course. At the second trial a huge eel-like monster appeared, which entered by one of the windows, crawled about among the furniture of the banqueting hall, and finally coiled itself round the body of the Countess. Still she showed no fear, and at a nod from the Earl the animal uncoiled itself and disappeared. In the third test an intimate friend of the Countess, long since dead, entered the room, and passing slowly by her went out at the other end. She showed not the slightest sign of fear, and the Earl felt satisfied that he could place his fate in her keeping, but he again warned her of his danger if she lost her presence of mind while he was in another shape. He then turned himself into a black bird, flew about the room, and perching on the Countess's shoulder commenced to sing. Suddenly a black cat appeared from under a chest, and made a spring at the bird; in an agony of fear for its safety the Countess threw up her arms to protect it and swooned away. When she came to she was alone, the bird and the cat had disappeared, and she never saw the Earl again."

It is said that he and his knights lie in an enchanted sleep, with their horses beside them, in a cave under the Rath on the hill of Mullaghmast, which stands, as the crow flies, five miles to the north of Kilkea Castle. Once in seven years they are allowed to issue forth; they gallop round the Curragh, thence across country to Kilkea Castle, where they re-enter the haunted wing, and then return to the Rath of Mullaghmast. The Earl is easily recognised as he is mounted on a white charger shod with silver shoes;

when these shoes are worn out the enchantment will be broken, and he will issue forth, drive the foes of Ireland from the land, and reign for a seven times seven number of years over the vast estates of his ancestors.

Shortly before '98 he was seen on the Curragh by a blacksmith who was crossing it in an ass-cart from Athgarvan to Kildare. A fairy blast overtook him, and he had just time to say, "God speed ye Gentlemen" to the invisible "Good People," when he heard horses galloping up behind him; pulling to one side of the road he looked back and was terrified at seeing a troop of knights, fully armed, led by one on a white horse. The leader halted his men, and riding up to the blacksmith asked him to examine his shoes. Almost helpless from fear he stumbled out of the ass-cart and looked at each shoe, which was of silver, and then informed the knight that all the nails were sound. The knight thanked him, rejoined his troop, and galloped off. The blacksmith in a half-dazed state hastened on to Kildare, where he entered a public-house, ordered a noggin of whisky, and drank it neat. When he had thoroughly come to himself he told the men that were present what had happened to him on the Curragh; one old man who had listened to him said: "By the mortial! man, ye are after seeing 'Gerod Earla.'" This fully explained the mystery. Gerod Earla, or Earl Gerald, is the name by which the Wizard Earl is known by the peasantry.

One other legend is told in connection with the Wizard Earl of a considerably later date. It is said that a farmer was returning from a fair in Athy late one evening in the direction of Ballintore, and when passing within view of the Rath of Mullaghmast he was astonished to see a bright light apparently issuing from it. Dismounting from his car he went to investigate. On approaching the Rath he noticed that the light was proceeding from a cave in which were sleeping several men in armour, with their horses beside them. He cautiously crept up to the entrance, and seeing that neither man nor beast stirred he grew bolder and entered the chamber; he then examined the saddlery on the horses, and the armour of the men, and plucking up courage began slowly to draw a sword from its sheath; as he did so the owner's head began to rise, and he heard a voice in Irish say, "Is the time yet come?" In terror the farmer, as he shoved the sword back, replied, "It is not, your Honour," and then fled from the place.

It is said that if the farmer had only completely unsheathed the sword the enchantment would have been broken, and the Earl would have come to his own again.

In 1642 Wallstown Castle, the seat of the Wall family, in County Cork, was burnt down by the Cromwellian troops, and Colonel Wall, the head of the family, was captured and imprisoned in Cork jail, where he died. One of the defenders during the siege was a man named Henry Bennett, who was killed while fighting. His ghost was often seen about the place for years after his death. His dress was of a light colour, and he wore a white hat, while in his hand he carried a pole, which he used to place across the road near the Castle to stop travellers; on a polite request to remove the pole he would withdraw it, and laugh heartily. A caretaker in the place named Philip Coughlan used frequently to be visited by this apparition. He came generally about supper time, and while Coughlan and his wife were seated at table he would shove the pole through the window; Coughlan would beg him to go away and not interfere with a poor hard-worked man; the pole would then be withdrawn, with a hearty laugh from the ghost.

In the Parish Church of Ardtrea, near Cookstown, is a marble monument and inscription in memory of Thomas Meredith, D.D., who had been a Fellow of Trinity College, Dublin, and for six years rector of the parish. He died, according to the words of the inscription, on 2nd May 1819, as a result of "a sudden and awful visitation." A local legend explains this "visitation," by stating that a ghost haunted the rectory, the visits of which had caused his family and servants to leave the house. The rector had tried to shoot it but failed; then he was told to use a silver bullet; he did so, and next morning was found dead at his hall-door while a hideous object like a devil made horrid noises out of any window the servant man approached. This man was advised by some Roman Catholic neighbours to get the priest, who would "lay" the thing. The priest arrived, and with the help of a jar of whisky the ghost became quite civil, till the last glass in the jar, which the priest was about to empty out for himself, whereupon the ghost or devil made himself as thin and long as a Lough Neagh eel, and slipped himself into the jar to get the last drops. But the priest put the cork into its place and hammered it in, and, making the sign of the Cross on it, he had the evil thing secured. It was buried in the cellar of the rectory, where on some nights it can still be heard calling to be let out.

A story of a phantom rat, which comes from Limerick, is only one of many which show the popular Irish belief in hauntings by various animals. Many years ago, the legend runs, a young man was making frantic and unacceptable love to a girl. At last, one day when he was following her in the street, she turned on him and, pointing to a rat which some boys had just killed, said, "I'd as soon marry that rat as you." He took her cruel words so much to heart that he pined away and died. After his death the girl was haunted at night by a rat, and in spite of the constant watch of her mother and sisters she was more than once bitten. The priest was called in and could do nothing, so she determined to emigrate. A coasting vessel was about to start for Queenstown, and her friends, collecting what money they could, managed to get her on board. The ship had just cast off from the quay, when shouts and screams were heard up the street. The crowd scattered, and a huge rat with fiery eyes galloped down to the quay.

129

It sat upon the edge screaming hate, sprang off, and did not reappear. After that, we are told, the girl was never again haunted.

A legend of the Tirawley family relates how a former Lord Tirawley, who was a very wild and reckless man, was taken from this world. One evening, it is said, just as the nobleman was preparing for a night's carouse, a carriage drove up to his door, a stranger asked to see him and, after a long private conversation, drove away as mysteriously as he had come. Whatever words had passed they had a wonderful effect on the gay lord, for his ways were immediately changed, and he lived the life of a reformed man. As time went on the effect of whatever awful warning the mysterious visitor had given him wore off, and he began to live a life even more wild and reckless than before. On the anniversary of the visit he was anxious and gloomy, but he tried to make light of it. The day passed, and at night there was high revelry in the banqueting hall. Outside it was wet and stormy, when just before midnight the sound of wheels was heard in the courtyard. All the riot stopped; the servants opened the door in fear and trembling: outside stood a huge dark coach with four black horses. The "fearful guest" entered and beckoned to Lord Tirawley, who followed him to a room off the hall. The friends, sobered by fear, saw through the door the stranger drawing a ship on the wall; the piece of wall then detached itself and the ship grew solid, the stranger climbed into it, and Lord Tirawley followed without a struggle. The vessel then sailed away into the night, and neither it nor its occupants were ever seen again.

The above tale is a good example of how a legend will rise superior to the ordinary humdrum facts of life, for it strikes us at once that the gloomy spectre went to unnecessary trouble in constructing a ship, even though the task proved so simple to his gifted hands. But the coach was at the door, and surely it would have been less troublesome to have used it.

A strange legend is told of a house in the Boyne valley. It is said that the occupant of the guest chamber was always wakened on the first night of his visit, then he would see a pale light and the shadow of a skeleton "climbing the wall like a huge spider." It used to crawl out on to the ceiling, and when it reached the middle would materialise into apparent bones, holding on by its hands and feet; it would break in pieces, and first the skull and then the other bones would fall on the floor. One person had the courage to get up and try to seize a bone, but his hand passed through to the carpet though the heap was visible for a few seconds.

The following story can hardly be called *legendary*, though it may certainly be termed ancestral. The writer's name is not given, but he is described as a rector and Rural Dean in the late Established Church of Ireland, and a Justice of the Peace for two counties. It has this added interest that it was told to Queen Victoria by the Marchioness of Ely.

"Loftus Hall, in County Wexford, was built on the site of a stronghold erected by Raymond, one of Strongbow's followers. His descendants forfeited it in 1641, and the property subsequently fell into the hands of the Loftus family, one of whom built the house and other buildings. About the middle of the eighteenth century, there lived at Loftus Hall Charles Tottenham, a member of the Irish Parliament, known to fame as 'Tottenham and his Boots,' owing to his historic ride to the Irish capital in order to give the casting vote in a motion which saved £80,000 to the Irish Treasury.

"The second son, Charles Tottenham, had two daughters, Elizabeth and Anne, to the latter of whom our story relates. He came to live at Loftus Hall, the old baronial residence of the family, with his second wife and the two above-mentioned daughters of his first wife. Loftus Hall was an old rambling mansion, with no pretence to beauty: passages that led nowhere, large dreary rooms, small closets, various unnecessary nooks and corners, panelled or wainscotted walls, and a *tapestry chamber*. Here resided at the time my story commences Charles Tottenham, his second wife and his daughter Anne: Elizabeth, his second daughter, having been married. The father was a cold austere man; the stepmother such as that unamiable relation is generally represented to be. What and how great the state of lonely solitude and depression of mind of poor Anne must have been in such a place, without neighbours or any home sympathy, may easily be imagined.

"One wet and stormy night, as they sat in the large drawing-room, they were startled by a loud knocking at the outer gate, a most surprising and unusual occurrence. Presently the servant announced that a young gentleman on horseback was there requesting lodging and shelter. He had lost his way, his horse was knocked up, and he had been guided by the only light which he had seen. The stranger was admitted and refreshed, and proved himself to be an agreeable companion and a finished gentleman— far too agreeable for the lone scion of the House of Tottenham, for a sad and mournful tale follows, and one whose strange results continued almost to the present day.

"Much mystery has involved the story at the present point, and in truth the matter was left in such silence and obscurity, that, but for the acts of her who was the chief sufferer in it through several generations, nothing would now be known. The fact, I believe, was—which was not unnatural under the circumstances— that this lonely girl formed a strong attachment to this gallant youth chance had brought to her door, which was warmly returned. The father, as was his stern nature, was obdurate, and the wife no solace to her as she was a step-mother. It is only an instance of the refrain of the old ballad, 'He loved, and he rode away'; he had youth and friends, and stirring scenes, and soon forgot his passing attach-ment. Poor Anne's reason gave way.

"The fact is but too true, she became a confirmed maniac, and had to be confined for the rest of her life in the tapestried cham-ber before mentioned, and in which she died. A strange legend was at once invented to account for this calamity: it tells how the horseman proved such an agreeable acquisition that he was invited to remain some days, and made himself quite at home, and as they were now four in number whist was proposed in the evenings. The stranger, however, with Anne as his partner, invariably won every point; the old couple never had the smallest success. One night, when poor Anne was in great delight at winning so constantly, she dropped a ring on the floor, and, suddenly diving under the table to recover it, was terrified to see that her agreeable partner had an unmistakably cloven foot. Her screams made him aware of her discovery, and he at once vanished in a thunder-clap leaving a brimstone smell behind him. The poor girl never recovered from the shock, lapsed from one fit into another, and was carried to the tapestry room from which she never came forth alive.

"This story of his Satanic majesty got abroad, and many tales are told of how he continued to visit and disturb the house. The noises, the apparitions, and disturbances were innumerable, and greatly distressed old Charles Tottenham, his wife, and servants. It is said that they finally determined to call in the services of their parish priest, a Father Broders, who, armed with all the exorcisms of the Church, succeeded in confining the operations of the evil spirit to one room—the tapestry room.

"Here, then, we have traced from the date of the unhappy girl's misfortune that the house was disturbed by something supernatural, and that the family sought the aid of the parish priest to abate it, and further that the tapestry room was the scene of this visitation.

"But the matter was kept dark, all reference to poor Anne was avoided, and the belief was allowed to go abroad that it was Satan himself who disturbed the peace of the family. Her parents were ready to turn aside the keen edge of observation from her fate, preferring rather that it should be believed that they were haunted by the Devil, so that the story of her wrongs should sink into oblivion, and be classed as an old wives' tale of horns and hoofs. The harsh father and stepmother have long gone to the place appointed for all living. The Loftus branch of the family are in possession of the Hall. Yet poor Anne has kept her tapestried chamber by nearly the same means which compelled her parents to call in the aid of the parish priest so long ago.

"But to my tale: About the end of the last century my father was invited by Mrs. Tottenham to meet a large party at the Hall. He rode, as was then the custom in Ireland, with his pistols in his holsters. On arriving he found the house full, and Mrs. Tottenham apologised to him for being obliged to assign to him the tapestry chamber for the night, which, however, he gladly accepted, never having heard any of the stories connected with it.

"However, he had scarcely covered himself in the bed when suddenly something heavy leaped upon it, growling like a dog. The curtains were torn back, and the clothes stripped from the bed. Supposing that some of his companions were playing tricks, he called out that he would shoot them, and seizing a pistol he fired up the chimney, lest he should wound one of them. He then struck a light and searched the room diligently, but found no sign or mark of anyone, and the door locked as he had left it on retiring to rest. Next day he informed his hosts how he had been annoyed, but they could only say that they would not have put him in that room if they had had any other to offer him.

"Years passed on, when the Marquis of Ely went to the Hall to spend some time there. His valet was put to sleep in the tapestry chamber. In the middle of the night the whole family was aroused by his dreadful roars and screams, and he was found lying in another room in mortal terror. After some time he told them that, soon after he had lain himself down in bed, he was startled by the rattling of the curtains as they were torn back, and looking up he saw a tall lady by the bedside dressed in stiff brocaded silk; whereupon he rushed out of the room screaming with terror.

"Years afterwards I was brought by my father with the rest of the family to the Hall for the summer bathing. Attracted by the quaint look of the tapestry room, I at once chose it for my bedroom, being utterly ignorant of the stories connected with it. For some little time nothing out of the way happened. One night, however, I sat up much later than usual to finish an article in a magazine I was reading. The full moon was shining clearly in through two large windows, making all as clear as day. I was just about to get into bed, and, happening to glance towards the door, to my great surprise I saw it open quickly and noiselessly, and as quickly and noiselessly shut again, while the tall figure of a lady in a stiff dress passed slowly through the room to one of the curious closets already mentioned, which was in the opposite corner. I rubbed my eyes. Every possible explanation but the true one occurred to my mind, for the idea of a ghost did not for a moment enter my head. I quickly reasoned myself into a sound sleep and forgot the matter.

"The next night I again sat up late in my bedroom, preparing a gun and ammunition to go and shoot sea-birds early next morning, when the door again opened and shut in the same noiseless manner, and the same tall lady proceeded to cross the room quietly and deliberately as before towards the closet. I instantly rushed at her, and threw my right arm around her, exclaiming 'Ha! I have you now!' To my utter astonishment my arm passed through her and came with a thud against the bedpost, at which spot she then was. The figure quickened its pace, and as it passed the skirt of its dress lapped against the curtain and I marked distinctly the pattern of her gown—a stiff brocaded silk.

"The ghostly solution of the problem did not yet enter my mind. However, I told the story at breakfast next morning. My father, who had himself suffered from the lady's visit so long before, never said a word, and it passed as some folly of mine. So slight was the impression it made on me at the time that, though I slept many a night after in the room, I never thought of watching or looking out for anything.

"Years later I was again a guest at the Hall. The Marquis of Ely and his family, with a large retinue of servants, filled the house to overflowing. As I passed the housekeeper's room I heard the valet say: 'What! I to sleep in the tapestry chamber? Never! I will leave my lord's service before I sleep there!' At once my former experience in that room flashed upon my mind. I had never thought of it during the interval, and was still utterly ignorant of Anne Tottenham: so when the housekeeper was gone I spoke to the valet and said, 'Tell me why you will not sleep in the tapestry room, as I have a particular reason for asking.' He said, 'Is it possible that you do not know that Miss Tottenham passes through that room every night, and, dressed in a stiff flowered silk dress, enters the closet in the corner?' I replied that I had never heard a word of her till now, but that I had, a few years before, twice seen a figure exactly like what he had described, and passed my arm through her body. 'Yes,' said he, 'that was Miss Tottenham, and, as is well known, she was confined—mad—in that room, and died there, and, they say, was buried in that closet.'

"Time wore on and another generation arose, another owner possessed the property—the grandson of my friend. In the year 185-, he being then a child came with his mother, the Marchioness of Ely, and his tutor, the Rev. Charles Dale, to the Hall for the bathing season. Mr. Dale was no imaginative person—a solid, steady, highly educated English clergyman, who had never even heard the name of Miss Tottenham. The tapestry room was his bed-chamber. One day in the late autumn of that year I received a letter from the uncle of the Marquis, saying, 'Do tell me what it was you saw long ago in the tapestry chamber, for something strange must have happened to the Rev. Charles Dale, as he came to breakfast quite mystified. Something very strange must have occurred, but he will not tell us, seems quite nervous, and, in short, is determined to give up his tutorship and return to England. Every year something mysterious has happened to any person who slept in that room, but they always kept it close. Mr. D——, a Wexford gentleman, slept there a short while ago. He had a splendid dressing-case, fitted with gold and silver articles, which he left carefully locked on his table at night; in the morning he found the whole of its contents scattered about the room.'

"Upon hearing this I determined to write to the Rev. Charles Dale, then Incumbent of a parish near Dover, telling him what had occurred to myself in the room, and that the evidence of supernatural appearances there were so strong and continued for several generations, that I was anxious to put them together, and I would consider it a great favour if he would tell me if anything had happened to him in the room, and of what nature. He then for the first time mentioned the matter, and from his letter now before me I make the following extracts:

"'For three weeks I experienced no inconvenience from the lady, but one night, just before we were about to leave, I had sat up very late. It was just one o'clock when I retired to my bedroom, a very beautiful moonlight night. I locked my door, and saw that the shutters were properly fastened, as I did every night. I had not lain myself down more than about five minutes before something jumped on the bed making a growling noise; the bedclothes were pulled off though I strongly resisted the pull. I immediately sprang out of bed, lighted my candle, looked into the closet and under the bed, but saw nothing.'

"Mr. Dale goes on to say that he endeavoured to account for it in some such way as I had formerly done, having never up to that time heard one word of the lady and her doings in that room. He adds, 'I did not see the lady or hear any noise but the growling.'

"Here then is the written testimony of a beneficed English clergyman, occupying the responsible position of tutor to the young Marquis of Ely, a most sober-minded and unimpressionable man. He repeats in 1867 almost the very words of my father when detailing his experience in that room in 1790—a man of whose existence he had never been cognisant, and therefore utterly ignorant of Miss Tottenham's doings in that room nearly eighty years before.

"In the autumn of 1868 I was again in the locality, at Dunmore, on the opposite side of the Waterford Estuary. I went across to see the old place and what alterations Miss Tottenham had forced the proprietors to make in the tapestry chamber. I found that the closet into which the poor lady had always vanished was taken away, the room enlarged, and two additional windows put in: the old tapestry had gone and a billiard-table occupied the site of poor Anne's bed. I took the old housekeeper aside, and asked her to tell me how Miss Tottenham bore these changes in her apartment. She looked quite frightened and most anxious to avoid the question, but at length hurriedly replied, 'Oh, Master George! don't talk about her: last night she made a horrid noise knocking the billiard-balls about!'

"I have thus traced with strict accuracy this most real and true tale, from the days of 'Tottenham and his Boots' to those of his great-great-grandson. Loftus Hall has since been wholly rebuilt, but I have not heard whether poor Anne Tottenham has condescended to visit it, or is wholly banished at last."

CHAPTER X

Mistaken Identity: Conclusion

WE HAVE GIVEN various instances of ghostly phenomena
wherein the witnesses have failed at first to realise that what they
saw partook in any way of the abnormal. There are also many
cases where a so-called ghost has turned out to be something
very ordinary. Though more often than not such incidents are
of a very trivial or self-explanatory nature (*e.g.* where a sheep
in a churchyard almost paralysed a midnight wayfarer till he
summoned up courage to investigate), there are many which
have an interest of their own and which often throw into promi-
nence the extraordinary superstitions and beliefs which exist in
a country.

Our first story, which is sent us by Mr. De Lacy of Dublin, deals
with an incident that occurred in the early part of last century.
An epidemic which was then rife in the city was each day taking its toll of the unhappy citizens. The wife of a man living
in Merrion Square was stricken down and hastily buried in a
churchyard in Donnybrook which is now closed. On the night
after the funeral one of the city police, or "Charlies" as they were
then called, passed through the churchyard on his rounds. When
nearing the centre he was alarmed to hear a sound coming from
a grave close at hand, and turning, saw a white apparition sit
up and address him. This was all he waited for; with a shriek he
dropped his lantern and staff and made off as fast as his legs

139

would carry him. The apparition thereupon took up the lamp and staff, and walked to Merrion Square to the house of mourning, was admitted by the servants, and to the joy of the whole household was found to be the object of their grief returned, Alcestis-like, from the grave. It seems that the epidemic was so bad that the bodies of the victims were interred hastily and without much care: the unfortunate lady had really been in a state of coma or trance, and as the grave was lightly covered, when she came to she was able to force her way up, and seeing the "Charlie" passing, she called for assistance.

An occurrence which at first had all the appearance of partaking of the supernormal, and which was afterwards found to have a curious explanation, is related by Dean Ovenden of St. Patrick's Cathedral, Dublin. "At Dunluce Rectory, Co. Antrim," he writes, "I had a strange experience. There was a force-pump attached to the back wall of the house, and many people drew water from it, as it was better than any obtained at that time in Bushmills. We used to notice, when going to bed, the sound of someone working the pump. All the servants denied that they ever used the pump between 11 P.M. and 12 midnight. I often looked out of the back window when I heard the pump going, but could not see anyone. I tied threads to the handle, but although they were found unbroken in the morning the pumping continued, sometimes only for three or four moves of the handle. On many nights no pumping was heard. The man-servant sat up with a gun and the dog, but he neither saw nor heard anything. We gave it up as a bad job, and still the pumping went on. After about two years of this experience, I was one night alone in the house. It was a calm and frosty night and I went to bed about 11:30 P.M. and lay awake; suddenly the pump began to work with great clearness, and mechanically I counted the strokes: they were exactly twelve. I exclaimed, 'The dining-room clock!' I sprang from bed and went down, and found that the clock was fast, as it showed two minutes past twelve o'clock. I set back the hands to 11:55 and lay in bed again, and soon the pumper began as usual. The explanation was that the vibration of the rising and falling hammer was carried up to the bedroom by the wall, but the sound of the bell was never heard. I found afterwards that the nights when there was no pumping were always windy."

A man was walking along a country lane at night and as he was coming round a bend he saw a coffin on the road in front of him. At first he thought it was a warning to him that he was soon to leave this world; but after some hesitation, he finally summoned up courage to give the thing a poke with his stick, when he found that the coffin was merely an outline of sea-weed which some passer-by had made. Whereupon he went on his way much relieved.

The unbeliever will state that rats or mice are more often than not the cause of so-called ghostly noises in a house. That, at any rate, instances have happened where one or other of these rodents has given rise to fear and trepidation in the inmates of a house or bedroom is proved by the following story from a Dublin lady. She tells how she was awakened by a most mysterious noise for which she could give no explanation. Overcome by fear, she was quite unable to get out of bed, and lay awake the rest of the night. When light came she got up: there was a big bath in the room, and in it she found a mouse which had been drowned in its efforts to get out. So her haunting was caused by what we may perhaps call a ghost in the making.

The devil is very real to the average countryman in Ireland. He has given his name to many spots which for some reason or other have gained some ill-repute—the Devil's Elbow, a very nasty bit of road down in Kerry, is an instance in point. The following story shows how prevalent the idea is that the devil is an active agent in the affairs of this world.

A family living at Ardee, Co. Louth, were one night sitting reading in the parlour. The two maids were amusing themselves at some card game in the kitchen. Suddenly there was a great commotion and the two girls—both from the country—burst into the sitting-room, pale with fright, and almost speechless. When they had recovered a certain amount, they were asked what was the matter; the cook immediately exclaimed, "Oh, sir! the devil, the devil, he knocked three times at the window and frightened us dreadfully, and we had just time to throw the cards into the fire and run in here before he got us." One of the family, on hearing this, immediately went out to see what had caused all this trepidation, and found a swallow with a broken neck lying on the kitchen windowsill. The poor bird had evidently seen the light in the room, and in its efforts to get near it had broken its neck against the glass of the window.

An amusing account of a pseudo-haunting comes from County Tipperary, and shows how extraordinarily strong is the countryman's belief in supernatural phenomena. The incidents related occurred only a very short time ago. A farmer in the vicinity of Thurles died leaving behind him a young widow. The latter lived alone after her husband's death, and about three months after the funeral she was startled one night by loud knocking at the door. On opening the door she was shocked at seeing the outline of a man dressed in a shroud. In a solemn voice he asked her did she know who he was: on receiving a reply in the negative, he said that he was her late husband and that he wanted £10 to get into heaven. The terrified woman said she had not got the money, but promised to have it ready if he would call again the next night. The "apparition" agreed, then withdrew, and the distracted woman went to bed wondering how she was to raise the money. When morning came she did not take long in telling her friends of her experience, in the hope that they would be able to help her. Their advice, however, was that she should tell the police, and she did so. That night the "apparition" returned at the promised hour, and asked for his money. The amount was handed to him, and in a low sepulchral voice he said, "Now I leave this earth and go to heaven." Unfortunately, as he was leaving, a sergeant and a constable of the R. I. Constabulary stopped him, questioned him, and hauled him off to the barracks to spend the remainder of the night in the cell, where no doubt he decided that the haunting game has its trials.[1]

An occurrence of very much the same description took place in County Clare about three years ago. Again the departed husband returns to his sorrowing wife, sits by the fire with her, chatting no doubt of old times, and before he leaves for the other world is regaled with pig's head and plenty of whisky. The visit is repeated the next night, and a request made for money to play cards with down below: the wife willingly gives him the money. Again he comes, and again he borrows on the plea that he had lost the night before, but hoped to get better luck next time. On the woman telling a neighbour a watch was kept for the dead man's return, but he never came near the place again.

An account of a police-court trial which appeared in the *Irish Times* of 31st December 1913 emphasizes in a very marked degree the extraordinary grip that superstition has over some of the country people. A young woman was on her trial for stealing £300 from the brother of her employer, Patrick McFaul of Armagh. District Inspector Lowndes, in opening the case for the Crown, told the bench that the money had been taken out of the bank by McFaul to buy a holding, for the purchase of which negotiations were going on. The money was carelessly thrown

[1] *Evening Telegraph* for Dec. 10, 1913.

143

into a drawer in a bedroom, and left there till it would be wanted. A short time afterwards a fire broke out in the room, and a heap of ashes was all that was found in the drawer, though little else in the room besides a few clothes was injured. "The McFauls appeared to accept their loss with a complacency, which could only be accounted for by the idea they entertained that the money was destroyed through spiritual intervention—that there were ghosts in the question, and that the destruction of the money was to be taken as a warning directed against a matrimonial arrangement, into which Michael McFaul was about to enter." The accused girl was servant to the McFauls, who discharged her a few days after the fire: but before this she had been into Derry and spent a night there; during her stay she tried to change three £20 notes with the help of a friend. But change was refused, and she had to abandon the attempt. "If some of the money was burned, some of it was certainly in existence three days later, to the amount of £60. One thing was manifest, and that was that an incredible amount of superstition appeared to prevail amongst families in that neighbourhood when the loss of such a sum as this could be attributed to anything but larceny, and it could for a moment be suggested that it was due to spiritual intervention to indicate that a certain course should be abandoned."

Conclusion

The foregoing tales have been inserted, not in order that they may throw ridicule on the rest of the book, but that they may act as a wholesome corrective. If *all* ghost stories could be subjected to such rigid examination it is probable that the mystery in many of them would be capable of equally simple solution— yet a remnant would be left.

And here, though it may seem somewhat belated, we must offer an apology for the use of the terms "ghost" and "ghost story."

The book includes such different items as hauntings, death-warnings, visions, and hallucinations, some of which obviously can no more be attributed to discarnate spirits than can the present writer's power of guiding his pen along the lines of a page; whether others of these must be laid to the credit of such unseen influences is just the question. But in truth there was no other expression than "ghost stories" which we could have used, or which could have conveyed to our readers, within reasonable verbal limits, as they glanced at its cover, or at an advertisement of it, a general idea of the contents of this book. The day will certainly come when, before the steady advance of scientific investigation, and the consequent influencing of public opinion, the word "ghost" will be relegated to limbo, and its place taken by a number of expressions corresponding to the results obtained from the analysis of phenomena hitherto grouped under this collective title. That day is approaching. And so, though we have used the term throughout the pages of this book, it must not therefore be assumed that we necessarily believe in "ghosts," or that we are bound to the theory that all, or any, of the unusual happenings therein recorded are due to the action of visitants from the Otherworld.

We may now anticipate one or two possible points of criticism. It might be alleged that the publication of such a book as this would tend to show that the Irish nation was enslaved in superstition. Without stopping to review the question as to what should, or should not, be classed as "superstition," we would rejoin by gleefully pointing to a leading article in the *Irish Times* of Jan. 27, 1914, which gives a short account of a lecture by Mr. Lovett on the folklore of London. Folklore in London! in the metropolis of the stolid Englishman! The fact is that the Irish people are not one whit more superstitious than their cross-channel neighbours, while they are surely on a far higher level in this respect than many of the Continental nations. They *seem* to be more superstitious because (we speak without wishing to give any offence) the *popu-*

145

lar religion of the majority has incorporated certain elements which may be traced back to pre-Christian times; but that they *are* actually more superstitious we beg leave to doubt.

Another and more important series of objections is stated by one of our correspondents as follows. "I must confess that I can never reconcile with my conception of an All-Wise Creator the type of 'ghost' you are at present interested in; it seems to me incredible that the spirits of the departed should be permitted to return and indulge in the ghostly repertoire of jangling chains, gurgling, &c., apparently for the sole purpose of scaring housemaids and other timid or hysterical people." The first and most obvious remark on this is, that our correspondent has never read or heard a ghost story, save of the Christmas magazine type, else he would be aware that the above theatrical display is *not* an integral part of the "ghostly repertoire"; and also that persons, who are *not* housemaids, and who can *not* be classed as timid or hysterical, but who, on the other hand, are exceedingly sober-minded, courageous, and level-headed, have had experiences (and been frightened by them too!) which cannot be explained on ordinary grounds. But on the main point our correspondent is begging the question, or at least assuming as fully proved a conclusion which is very far from being so. Is he quite sure that the only explanation of these strange sights and weird noises is that they are brought about by the action of departed spirits (we naturally exclude cases of deliberate fraud, which in reality are very unusual)? And if so, what meaning would he put upon the word "spirits"? And even if it be granted that the phenomena are caused by the inhabitants of another world, why should it be impossible to accept such a theory, because of its *apparent* incompatibility with any conception of an All-Wise Creator, of whose workings we are so profoundly ignorant? Are there not many things in the material world which *to the limited human mind* of our correspondent must seem puzzling, meaningless, useless, and even harmful? He does not therefore condemn these offhand; he is content to suspend judgment, is he not? Why cannot he adopt the same attitude with respect to psychic phenomena? Our correspondent might here make the obvious retort that it is *we* who are begging the question, not he, because such happenings as are described in this book have no existence apart from the imaginative or inventive faculties of certain persons. This would be equivalent to saying bluntly that a considerable number of people in Ireland are either liars or fools, or both. This point we shall deal with later on.

Our correspondent belongs to a type which knows nothing at all about psychical research, and is not aware that some of the cleverest scientists and deepest thinkers of the day have interested themselves in such problems. They have not found the answer to many of them—goodness knows if they ever will this side of the grave—but at least they have helped to broaden and deepen our knowledge of ourselves, our surroundings, and our God. They have revealed to us profundities in human personality hitherto unsuspected, they have suggested means of communication between mind and mind almost incredible, and (in the writer's opinion at least) these points have a very important bearing on our conceptions of the final state of mankind in the world to come, and so they are preparing the way for that finer and more ethical conception of God and His Creation which will be the heritage of generations yet unborn. The materialist's day is far spent, and its sun nears the horizon.

Another objection to the study of the subjects dealt with in this book is that we are designedly left in ignorance of the unseen world by a Wise Creator, and therefore that it is grossly presumptuous, not to say impious, on the part of man to make any attempt to probe into questions which he has not been intended to study. Which is equivalent to saying that it is impious to ride a bicycle, because man was obviously created a pedestrian. This might be true if we were confined within a self-contained world which had, and could have, no connection with anything external to itself. But the very essence of our existence here is that the material and spiritual worlds interpenetrate, or rather that our little planet forms part of a boundless universe teeming with life and intelligence, yet lying in the hollow of God's hand. He alone is "Supernatural," and therefore Transcendent and Unknowable; all things in the universe are "natural," though very often they are beyond our normal experience, and as such are legitimate objects for man's research. Surely the potential energy in the human intellect will not allow it to remain at its present stage, but will continually urge it onwards and upwards. What limits God in His Providence has seen fit to put upon us we cannot tell, for every moment the horizon is receding, and our outlook becoming larger, though some still find it difficult to bring their eyesight to the focus consequently required. The marvellous of to-day is the commonplace of to-morrow: "our notion of what is natural grows with our greater knowledge."

Throughout the pages of this book we have, in general, avoided offering explanations of, or theories to account for, the different stories. Here something may be said on this point. As we have already pointed out, the expression "ghost stories" covers a multitude of different phenomena. Many of these may be explained as "hallucinations," which does not imply that they are simply the effect of imagination and nothing more. "The mind receives the hallucination as if it came through the channels of sense, and accordingly externalises the impression, seeking its source in the world outside itself, whereas in all hallucinations the source is within the mind, and is not derived from an impression received through the recognised organ of sense."[1]

Many of these hallucinations are termed *veridical*, or truth-telling, because they coincide with real events occurring to another person. Illustrations of this will be found in Chapter VI, from which it would appear that a dying person (though the power

---

[1] Prof. Sir W. Barrett, *Psychical Research*, p. 111.

is not necessarily confined to such) occasionally has the faculty of telepathically communicating with another; the latter receives the impression, and externalises it, and so "sees a ghost," to use the popular expression. Some hallucinations are *auditory, i.e.* sounds are heard which apparently do not correspond to any objective reality. Incomprehensible though it may appear, it may be possible for sounds, and very loud ones too, to be heard by one or more persons, the said sounds being purely hallucinatory, and not causing any disturbance in the atmosphere.

Some of the incidents may be explained as due to telepathy, that mysterious power by which mind can communicate with mind, though what telepathy is, or through what medium it is propagated, no one can tell as yet. Belief in this force is increasing, because, as Professor Sir W. Barrett remarks: "Hostility to a new idea arises largely from its being unrelated to existing knowledge," and, as telepathy seems to the ordinary person to be analogous to wireless telegraphy, it is therefore accepted, or at least not laughed at, though how far the analogy really holds good is not at all certain.

Again there is the question of haunted houses and places, to accounts of which the first five chapters of this book are devoted. The actual evidence for many of these may not come up to the rigorous standard set by the S.P.R., but it is beyond all doubt that persons who are neither fools, liars, nor drunkards firmly believe that they have seen and heard the things related in these chapters (not to speak of Chapters VI-VIII), or that they have been told such by those in whose statements they place implicit confidence; while so certain are they that they are telling the truth that they have not only written down the stories for the compilers, but have given their names and addresses as well, though not always for publication. Can we contemptuously fling aside such a weight of evidence as unworthy of even a cursory examination? This would hardly be a rational attitude to adopt. Various theories to account for these strange hauntings have been formulated, which may be found on pp. 199-200 of Sir William Barrett's *Psychical Research*, and so need not be given here.

Yet, when all is said and done, the very formulating of theories, so far from solving problems, only raises further and more complex ones, perhaps the greatest of which is, Have the spirits of the departed anything to do with the matter? As we have shown, we hope with success, in the preceding paragraphs, many "ghosts" have no necessary connection with the denizens of the unseen world, but may be explained as being due to laws of nature which at present are very obscure. Does this hold good of all "ghosts," or are some of them to be placed to the credit of those who have passed beyond the veil, or perhaps to spirits, good or evil, which have never been incarnate? That is the problem for the future, for in the present state of our knowledge it would be premature to give a direct answer, either positive or negative.

This book was written with a twofold purpose: first, that of entertaining our readers, in which we trust we have been successful; secondly, to stimulate thought. For, strange though it may seem, authenticated "ghost stories" have a certain educative value. Taking them at their lowest they suggest inquiry into the strange workings of the human mind: at their highest how many strange lines of inquiry do they not suggest? For it is obvious that we have now arrived at one of those interesting periods in the history of human thought which might be described as the return of the pendulum. We are in the process of emerging from a very materialistic age, when men either refused to believe anything that was contrary to their normal experience, or else leavened their spiritual doctrines and beliefs with the leaven of materialism. The pendulum has swung to its highest point in this respect, and is now commencing to return, so perhaps the intellectual danger of the future will be that men, instead of believing too little, will believe too much. Now is the time for laying a careful foundation. Psychical research, spiritualism, and the like, are not ends in themselves, they are only means to an end. At the present state of thought, the transition from the old to the new, from the lower to the higher, it is inevitable that there must be confusion and doubt, and the earnest thinker must be prepared to suspend judgment on many points; but at a later stage, when all absurdity, error, and fraud, now so closely connected with psychical research in its various branches, will have been swept away, Truth will emerge and lift the human race to a purer and loftier conception of God and His universe.

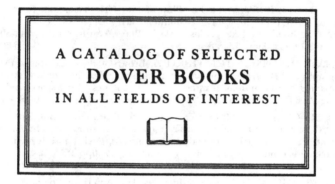

A CATALOG OF SELECTED
DOVER BOOKS
IN ALL FIELDS OF INTEREST

A CATALOG OF SELECTED DOVER
BOOKS IN ALL FIELDS OF INTEREST

100 BEST-LOVED POEMS, Edited by Philip Smith. "The Passionate Shepherd to His Love," "Shall I compare thee to a summer's day?" "Death, be not proud," "The Raven," "The Road Not Taken," plus works by Blake, Wordsworth, Byron, Shelley, Keats, many others. 96pp. 5³⁄₁₆ x 8¼. 0-486-28553-7

100 SMALL HOUSES OF THE THIRTIES, Brown-Blodgett Company. Exterior photographs and floor plans for 100 charming structures. Illustrations of models accompanied by descriptions of interiors, color schemes, closet space, and other amenities. 200 illustrations. 112pp. 8⅜ x 11. 0-486-44131-8

1000 TURN-OF-THE-CENTURY HOUSES: With Illustrations and Floor Plans, Herbert C. Chivers. Reproduced from a rare edition, this showcase of homes ranges from cottages and bungalows to sprawling mansions. Each house is meticulously illustrated and accompanied by complete floor plans. 256pp. 9⅜ x 12¼.
0-486-45596-3

101 GREAT AMERICAN POEMS, Edited by The American Poetry & Literacy Project. Rich treasury of verse from the 19th and 20th centuries includes works by Edgar Allan Poe, Robert Frost, Walt Whitman, Langston Hughes, Emily Dickinson, T. S. Eliot, other notables. 96pp. 5³⁄₁₆ x 8¼. 0-486-40158-8

101 GREAT SAMURAI PRINTS, Utagawa Kuniyoshi. Kuniyoshi was a master of the warrior woodblock print — and these 18th-century illustrations represent the pinnacle of his craft. Full-color portraits of renowned Japanese samurais pulse with movement, passion, and remarkably fine detail. 112pp. 8⅜ x 11. 0-486-46523-3

ABC OF BALLET, Janet Grosser. Clearly worded, abundantly illustrated little guide defines basic ballet-related terms: arabesque, battement, pas de chat, relevé, sissonne, many others. Pronunciation guide included. Excellent primer. 48pp. 4³⁄₁₆ x 5¾.
0-486-40871-X

ACCESSORIES OF DRESS: An Illustrated Encyclopedia, Katherine Lester and Bess Viola Oerke. Illustrations of hats, veils, wigs, cravats, shawls, shoes, gloves, and other accessories enhance an engaging commentary that reveals the humor and charm of the many-sided story of accessorized apparel. 644 figures and 59 plates. 608pp. 6 ⅛ x 9¼.
0-486-43378-1

ADVENTURES OF HUCKLEBERRY FINN, Mark Twain. Join Huck and Jim as their boyhood adventures along the Mississippi River lead them into a world of excitement, danger, and self-discovery. Humorous narrative, lyrical descriptions of the Mississippi valley, and memorable characters. 224pp. 5³⁄₁₆ x 8¼. 0-486-28061-6

ALICE STARMORE'S BOOK OF FAIR ISLE KNITTING, Alice Starmore. A noted designer from the region of Scotland's Fair Isle explores the history and techniques of this distinctive, stranded-color knitting style and provides copious illustrated instructions for 14 original knitwear designs. 208pp. 8⅜ x 10⅞. 0-486-47218-3

Browse over 9,000 books at www.doverpublications.com

CATALOG OF DOVER BOOKS

ALICE'S ADVENTURES IN WONDERLAND, Lewis Carroll. Beloved classic about a little girl lost in a topsy-turvy land and her encounters with the White Rabbit, March Hare, Mad Hatter, Cheshire Cat, and other delightfully improbable characters. 42 illustrations by Sir John Tenniel. 96pp. 5¾6 x 8¼.　　　　0-486-27543-4

AMERICA'S LIGHTHOUSES: An Illustrated History, Francis Ross Holland. Profusely illustrated fact-filled survey of American lighthouses since 1716. Over 200 stations — East, Gulf, and West coasts, Great Lakes, Hawaii, Alaska, Puerto Rico, the Virgin Islands, and the Mississippi and St. Lawrence Rivers. 240pp. 8 x 10¾.
0-486-25576-X

AN ENCYCLOPEDIA OF THE VIOLIN, Alberto Bachmann. Translated by Frederick H. Martens. Introduction by Eugene Ysaye. First published in 1925, this renowned reference remains unsurpassed as a source of essential information, from construction and evolution to repertoire and technique. Includes a glossary and 73 illustrations. 496pp. 6½ x 9¼.　　　　0-486-46618-3

ANIMALS: 1,419 Copyright-Free Illustrations of Mammals, Birds, Fish, Insects, etc., Selected by Jim Harter. Selected for its visual impact and ease of use, this outstanding collection of wood engravings presents over 1,000 species of animals in extremely lifelike poses. Includes mammals, birds, reptiles, amphibians, fish, insects, and other invertebrates. 284pp. 9 x 12.　　　　0-486-23766-4

THE ANNALS, Tacitus. Translated by Alfred John Church and William Jackson Brodribb. This vital chronicle of Imperial Rome, written by the era's great historian, spans A.D. 14-68 and paints incisive psychological portraits of major figures, from Tiberius to Nero. 416pp. 5¾6 x 8¼.　　　　0-486-45236-0

ANTIGONE, Sophocles. Filled with passionate speeches and sensitive probing of moral and philosophical issues, this powerful and often-performed Greek drama reveals the grim fate that befalls the children of Oedipus. Footnotes. 64pp. 5¾6 x 8 ¼.　　　　0-486-27804-2

ART DECO DECORATIVE PATTERNS IN FULL COLOR, Christian Stoll. Reprinted from a rare 1910 portfolio, 160 sensuous and exotic images depict a breathtaking array of florals, geometrics, and abstracts — all elegant in their stark simplicity. 64pp. 8⅜ x 11.　　　　0-486-44862-2

THE ARTHUR RACKHAM TREASURY: 86 Full-Color Illustrations, Arthur Rackham. Selected and Edited by Jeff A. Menges. A stunning treasury of 86 full-page plates span the famed English artist's career, from *Rip Van Winkle* (1905) to masterworks such as *Undine, A Midsummer Night's Dream*, and *Wind in the Willows* (1939). 96pp. 8⅜ x 11.
0-486-44685-9

THE AUTHENTIC GILBERT & SULLIVAN SONGBOOK, W. S. Gilbert and A. S. Sullivan. The most comprehensive collection available, this songbook includes selections from every one of Gilbert and Sullivan's light operas. Ninety-two numbers are presented uncut and unedited, and in their original keys. 410pp. 9 x 12.
0-486-23482-7

THE AWAKENING, Kate Chopin. First published in 1899, this controversial novel of a New Orleans wife's search for love outside a stifling marriage shocked readers. Today, it remains a first-rate narrative with superb characterization. New introductory Note. 128pp. 5¾6 x 8¼.　　　　0-486-27786-0

BASIC DRAWING, Louis Priscilla. Beginning with perspective, this commonsense manual progresses to the figure in movement, light and shade, anatomy, drapery, composition, trees and landscape, and outdoor sketching. Black-and-white illustrations throughout. 128pp. 8⅜ x 11.　　　　0-486-45815-6

Browse over 9,000 books at www.doverpublications.com

THE BATTLES THAT CHANGED HISTORY, Fletcher Pratt. Historian profiles 16 crucial conflicts, ancient to modern, that changed the course of Western civilization. Gripping accounts of battles led by Alexander the Great, Joan of Arc, Ulysses S. Grant, other commanders. 27 maps. 352pp. 5⅜ x 8½. 0-486-41129-X

BEETHOVEN'S LETTERS, Ludwig van Beethoven. Edited by Dr. A. C. Kalischer. Features 457 letters to fellow musicians, friends, greats, patrons, and literary men. Reveals musical thoughts, quirks of personality, insights, and daily events. Includes 15 plates. 410pp. 5⅜ x 8½. 0-486-22769-3

BERNICE BOBS HER HAIR AND OTHER STORIES, F. Scott Fitzgerald. This brilliant anthology includes 6 of Fitzgerald's most popular stories: "The Diamond as Big as the Ritz," the title tale, "The Offshore Pirate," "The Ice Palace," "The Jelly Bean," and "May Day." 176pp. 5⅜ x 8½. 0-486-47049-0

BESLER'S BOOK OF FLOWERS AND PLANTS: 73 Full-Color Plates from Hortus Eystettensis, 1613, Basilius Besler. Here is a selection of magnificent plates from the *Hortus Eystettensis,* which vividly illustrated and identified the plants, flowers, and trees that thrived in the legendary German garden at Eichstätt. 80pp. 8⅜ x 11. 0-486-46005-3

THE BOOK OF KELLS, Edited by Blanche Cirker. Painstakingly reproduced from a rare facsimile edition, this volume contains full-page decorations, portraits, illustrations, plus a sampling of textual leaves with exquisite calligraphy and ornamentation. 32 full-color illustrations. 32pp. 9⅜ x 12¼. 0-486-24345-1

THE BOOK OF THE CROSSBOW: With an Additional Section on Catapults and Other Siege Engines, Ralph Payne-Gallwey. Fascinating study traces history and use of crossbow as military and sporting weapon, from Middle Ages to modern times. Also covers related weapons: balistas, catapults, Turkish bows, more. Over 240 illustrations. 400pp. 7¼ x 10⅛. 0-486-28720-3

THE BUNGALOW BOOK: Floor Plans and Photos of 112 Houses, 1910, Henry L. Wilson. Here are 112 of the most popular and economic blueprints of the early 20th century — plus an illustration or photograph of each completed house. A wonderful time capsule that still offers a wealth of valuable insights. 160pp. 8⅜ x 11. 0-486-45104-6

THE CALL OF THE WILD, Jack London. A classic novel of adventure, drawn from London's own experiences as a Klondike adventurer, relating the story of a heroic dog caught in the brutal life of the Alaska Gold Rush. Note. 64pp. 5³⁄₁₆ x 8¼. 0-486-26472-6

CANDIDE, Voltaire. Edited by Francois-Marie Arouet. One of the world's great satires since its first publication in 1759. Witty, caustic skewering of romance, science, philosophy, religion, government — nearly all human ideals and institutions. 112pp. 5³⁄₁₆ x 8¼. 0-486-26689-3

CELEBRATED IN THEIR TIME: Photographic Portraits from the George Grantham Bain Collection, Edited by Amy Pastan. With an Introduction by Michael Carlebach. Remarkable portrait gallery features 112 rare images of Albert Einstein, Charlie Chaplin, the Wright Brothers, Henry Ford, and other luminaries from the worlds of politics, art, entertainment, and industry. 128pp. 8⅜ x 11. 0-486-46754-6

CHARIOTS FOR APOLLO: The NASA History of Manned Lunar Spacecraft to 1969, Courtney G. Brooks, James M. Grimwood, and Loyd S. Swenson, Jr. This illustrated history by a trio of experts is the definitive reference on the Apollo spacecraft and lunar modules. It traces the vehicles' design, development, and operation in space. More than 100 photographs and illustrations. 576pp. 6¾ x 9¼. 0-486-46756-2

Browse over 9,000 books at www.doverpublications.com

A CHRISTMAS CAROL, Charles Dickens. This engrossing tale relates Ebenezer Scrooge's ghostly journeys through Christmases past, present, and future and his ultimate transformation from a harsh and grasping old miser to a charitable and compassionate human being. 80pp. 5³⁄₁₆ x 8¼. 0-486-26865-9

COMMON SENSE, Thomas Paine. First published in January of 1776, this highly influential landmark document clearly and persuasively argued for American separation from Great Britain and paved the way for the Declaration of Independence. 64pp. 5³⁄₁₆ x 8¼. 0-486-29602-4

THE COMPLETE SHORT STORIES OF OSCAR WILDE, Oscar Wilde. Complete texts of "The Happy Prince and Other Tales," "A House of Pomegranates," "Lord Arthur Savile's Crime and Other Stories," "Poems in Prose," and "The Portrait of Mr. W. H." 208pp. 5³⁄₁₆ x 8¼. 0-486-45216-6

COMPLETE SONNETS, William Shakespeare. Over 150 exquisite poems deal with love, friendship, the tyranny of time, beauty's evanescence, death, and other themes in language of remarkable power, precision, and beauty. Glossary of archaic terms. 80pp. 5³⁄₁₆ x 8¼. 0-486-26686-9

THE COUNT OF MONTE CRISTO: Abridged Edition, Alexandre Dumas. Falsely accused of treason, Edmond Dantès is imprisoned in the bleak Chateau d'If. After a hair-raising escape, he launches an elaborate plot to extract a bitter revenge against those who betrayed him. 448pp. 5³⁄₁₆ x 8¼. 0-486-45643-9

CRAFTSMAN BUNGALOWS: Designs from the Pacific Northwest, Yoho & Merritt. This reprint of a rare catalog, showcasing the charming simplicity and cozy style of Craftsman bungalows, is filled with photos of completed homes, plus floor plans and estimated costs. An indispensable resource for architects, historians, and illustrators. 112pp. 10 x 7. 0-486-46875-5

CRAFTSMAN BUNGALOWS: 59 Homes from "The Craftsman," Edited by Gustav Stickley. Best and most attractive designs from Arts and Crafts Movement publication — 1903–1916 — includes sketches, photographs of homes, floor plans, descriptive text. 128pp. 8¼ x 11. 0-486-25829-7

CRIME AND PUNISHMENT, Fyodor Dostoyevsky. Translated by Constance Garnett. Supreme masterpiece tells the story of Raskolnikov, a student tormented by his own thoughts after he murders an old woman. Overwhelmed by guilt and terror, he confesses and goes to prison. 480pp. 5³⁄₁₆ x 8¼. 0-486-41587-2

THE DECLARATION OF INDEPENDENCE AND OTHER GREAT DOCUMENTS OF AMERICAN HISTORY: 1775-1865, Edited by John Grafton. Thirteen compelling and influential documents: Henry's "Give Me Liberty or Give Me Death," Declaration of Independence, The Constitution, Washington's First Inaugural Address, The Monroe Doctrine, The Emancipation Proclamation, Gettysburg Address, more. 64pp. 5³⁄₁₆ x 8¼. 0-486-41124-9

THE DESERT AND THE SOWN: Travels in Palestine and Syria, Gertrude Bell. "The female Lawrence of Arabia," Gertrude Bell wrote captivating, perceptive accounts of her travels in the Middle East. This intriguing narrative, accompanied by 160 photos, traces her 1905 sojourn in Lebanon, Syria, and Palestine. 368pp. 5⅜ x 8½.
0-486-46876-3

A DOLL'S HOUSE, Henrik Ibsen. Ibsen's best-known play displays his genius for realistic prose drama. An expression of women's rights, the play climaxes when the central character, Nora, rejects a smothering marriage and life in "a doll's house." 80pp. 5³⁄₁₆ x 8¼. 0-486-27062-9

DOOMED SHIPS: Great Ocean Liner Disasters, William H. Miller, Jr. Nearly 200 photographs, many from private collections, highlight tales of some of the vessels whose pleasure cruises ended in catastrophe: the *Morro Castle, Normandie, Andrea Doria, Europa,* and many others. 128pp. 8⅜ x 11¼. 0-486-45366-9

THE DORÉ BIBLE ILLUSTRATIONS, Gustave Doré. Detailed plates from the Bible: the Creation scenes, Adam and Eve, horrifying visions of the Flood, the battle sequences with their monumental crowds, depictions of the life of Jesus, 241 plates in all. 241pp. 9 x 12. 0-486-23004-X

DRAWING DRAPERY FROM HEAD TO TOE, Cliff Young. Expert guidance on how to draw shirts, pants, skirts, gloves, hats, and coats on the human figure, including folds in relation to the body, pull and crush, action folds, creases, more. Over 200 drawings. 48pp. 8¼ x 11. 0-486-45591-2

DUBLINERS, James Joyce. A fine and accessible introduction to the work of one of the 20th century's most influential writers, this collection features 15 tales, including a masterpiece of the short-story genre, "The Dead." 160pp. 5³⁄₁₆ x 8¼. 0-486-26870-5

EASY-TO-MAKE POP-UPS, Joan Irvine. Illustrated by Barbara Reid. Dozens of wonderful ideas for three-dimensional paper fun — from holiday greeting cards with moving parts to a pop-up menagerie. Easy-to-follow, illustrated instructions for more than 30 projects. 299 black-and-white illustrations. 96pp. 8⅜ x 11. 0-486-44622-0

EASY-TO-MAKE STORYBOOK DOLLS: A "Novel" Approach to Cloth Dollmaking, Sherralyn St. Clair. Favorite fictional characters come alive in this unique beginner's dollmaking guide. Includes patterns for Pollyanna, Dorothy from *The Wonderful Wizard of Oz,* Mary of *The Secret Garden,* plus easy-to-follow instructions, 263 black-and-white illustrations, and an 8-page color insert. 112pp. 8¼ x 11. 0-486-47360-0

EINSTEIN'S ESSAYS IN SCIENCE, Albert Einstein. Speeches and essays in accessible, everyday language profile influential physicists such as Niels Bohr and Isaac Newton. They also explore areas of physics to which the author made major contributions. 128pp. 5 x 8. 0-486-47011-3

EL DORADO: Further Adventures of the Scarlet Pimpernel, Baroness Orczy. A popular sequel to *The Scarlet Pimpernel,* this suspenseful story recounts the Pimpernel's attempts to rescue the Dauphin from imprisonment during the French Revolution. An irresistible blend of intrigue, period detail, and vibrant characterizations. 352pp. 5³⁄₁₆ x 8¼. 0-486-44026-5

ELEGANT SMALL HOMES OF THE TWENTIES: 99 Designs from a Competition, Chicago Tribune. Nearly 100 designs for five- and six-room houses feature New England and Southern colonials, Normandy cottages, stately Italianate dwellings, and other fascinating snapshots of American domestic architecture of the 1920s. 112pp. 9 x 12. 0-486-46910-7

THE ELEMENTS OF STYLE: The Original Edition, William Strunk, Jr. This is the book that generations of writers have relied upon for timeless advice on grammar, diction, syntax, and other essentials. In concise terms, it identifies the principal requirements of proper style and common errors. 64pp. 5⅜ x 8½. 0-486-44798-7

THE ELUSIVE PIMPERNEL, Baroness Orczy. Robespierre's revolutionaries find their wicked schemes thwarted by the heroic Pimpernel — Sir Percival Blakeney. In this thrilling sequel, Chauvelin devises a plot to eliminate the Pimpernel and his wife. 272pp. 5³⁄₁₆ x 8¼. 0-486-45464-9

AN ENCYCLOPEDIA OF BATTLES: Accounts of Over 1,560 Battles from 1479 B.C. to the Present, David Eggenberger. Essential details of every major battle in recorded history from the first battle of Megiddo in 1479 B.C. to Grenada in 1984. List of battle maps. 99 illustrations. 544pp. 6½ x 9¼. 0-486-24913-1

ENCYCLOPEDIA OF EMBROIDERY STITCHES, INCLUDING CREWEL, Marion Nichols. Precise explanations and instructions, clearly illustrated, on how to work chain, back, cross, knotted, woven stitches, and many more — 178 in all, including Cable Outline, Whipped Satin, and Eyelet Buttonhole. Over 1400 illustrations. 219pp. 8⅜ x 11¼. 0-486-22929-7

ENTER JEEVES: 15 Early Stories, P. G. Wodehouse. Splendid collection contains first 8 stories featuring Bertie Wooster, the deliciously dim aristocrat and Jeeves, his brainy, imperturbable manservant. Also, the complete Reggie Pepper (Bertie's prototype) series. 288pp. 5⅜ x 8½. 0-486-29717-9

ERIC SLOANE'S AMERICA: Paintings in Oil, Michael Wigley. With a Foreword by Mimi Sloane. Eric Sloane's evocative oils of America's landscape and material culture shimmer with immense historical and nostalgic appeal. This original hardcover collection gathers nearly a hundred of his finest paintings, with subjects ranging from New England to the American Southwest. 128pp. 10⅝ x 9.
0-486-46525-X

ETHAN FROME, Edith Wharton. Classic story of wasted lives, set against a bleak New England background. Superbly delineated characters in a hauntingly grim tale of thwarted love. Considered by many to be Wharton's masterpiece. 96pp. 5³⁄₁₆ x 8 ¼.
0-486-26690-7

THE EVERLASTING MAN, G. K. Chesterton. Chesterton's view of Christianity — as a blend of philosophy and mythology, satisfying intellect and spirit — applies to his brilliant book, which appeals to readers' heads as well as their hearts. 288pp. 5⅜ x 8½.
0-486-46036-3

THE FIELD AND FOREST HANDY BOOK, Daniel Beard. Written by a co-founder of the Boy Scouts, this appealing guide offers illustrated instructions for building kites, birdhouses, boats, igloos, and other fun projects, plus numerous helpful tips for campers. 448pp. 5³⁄₁₆ x 8¼. 0-486-46191-2

FINDING YOUR WAY WITHOUT MAP OR COMPASS, Harold Gatty. Useful, instructive manual shows would-be explorers, hikers, bikers, scouts, sailors, and survivalists how to find their way outdoors by observing animals, weather patterns, shifting sands, and other elements of nature. 288pp. 5⅜ x 8½. 0-486-40613-X

FIRST FRENCH READER: A Beginner's Dual-Language Book, Edited and Translated by Stanley Appelbaum. This anthology introduces 50 legendary writers — Voltaire, Balzac, Baudelaire, Proust, more — through passages from *The Red and the Black*, *Les Misérables, Madame Bovary*, and other classics. Original French text plus English translation on facing pages. 240pp. 5⅜ x 8½. 0-486-46178-5

FIRST GERMAN READER: A Beginner's Dual-Language Book, Edited by Harry Steinhauer. Specially chosen for their power to evoke German life and culture, these short, simple readings include poems, stories, essays, and anecdotes by Goethe, Hesse, Heine, Schiller, and others. 224pp. 5⅜ x 8½. 0-486-46179-3

FIRST SPANISH READER: A Beginner's Dual-Language Book, Angel Flores. Delightful stories, other material based on works of Don Juan Manuel, Luis Taboada, Ricardo Palma, other noted writers. Complete faithful English translations on facing pages. Exercises. 176pp. 5⅜ x 8½. 0-486-25810-6

CATALOG OF DOVER BOOKS

FIVE ACRES AND INDEPENDENCE, Maurice G. Kains. Great back-to-the-land classic explains basics of self-sufficient farming. The one book to get. 95 illustrations. 397pp. 5⅜ x 8½. 0-486-20974-1

FLAGG'S SMALL HOUSES: Their Economic Design and Construction, 1922, Ernest Flagg. Although most famous for his skyscrapers, Flagg was also a proponent of the well-designed single-family dwelling. His classic treatise features innovations that save space, materials, and cost. 526 illustrations. 160pp. 9⅜ x 12¼. 0-486-45197-6

FLATLAND: A Romance of Many Dimensions, Edwin A. Abbott. Classic of science (and mathematical) fiction — charmingly illustrated by the author — describes the adventures of A. Square, a resident of Flatland, in Spaceland (three dimensions), Lineland (one dimension), and Pointland (no dimensions). 96pp. 5³⁄₁₆ x 8¼. 0-486-27263-X

FRANKENSTEIN, Mary Shelley. The story of Victor Frankenstein's monstrous creation and the havoc it caused has enthralled generations of readers and inspired countless writers of horror and suspense. With the author's own 1831 introduction. 176pp. 5³⁄₁₆ x 8¼. 0-486-28211-2

THE GARGOYLE BOOK: 572 Examples from Gothic Architecture, Lester Burbank Bridaham. Dispelling the conventional wisdom that French Gothic architectural flourishes were born of despair or gloom, Bridaham reveals the whimsical nature of these creations and the ingenious artisans who made them. 572 illustrations. 224pp. 8⅜ x 11. 0-486-44754-5

THE GIFT OF THE MAGI AND OTHER SHORT STORIES, O. Henry. Sixteen captivating stories by one of America's most popular storytellers. Included are such classics as "The Gift of the Magi," "The Last Leaf," and "The Ransom of Red Chief." Publisher's Note. 96pp. 5³⁄₁₆ x 8¼. 0-486-27061-0

THE GOETHE TREASURY: Selected Prose and Poetry, Johann Wolfgang von Goethe. Edited, Selected, and with an Introduction by Thomas Mann. In addition to his lyric poetry, Goethe wrote travel sketches, autobiographical studies, essays, letters, and proverbs in rhyme and prose. This collection presents outstanding examples from each genre. 368pp. 5⅜ x 8½. 0-486-44780-4

GREAT EXPECTATIONS, Charles Dickens. Orphaned Pip is apprenticed to the dirty work of the forge but dreams of becoming a gentleman — and one day finds himself in possession of "great expectations." Dickens' finest novel. 400pp. 5³⁄₁₆ x 8¼. 0-486-41586-4

GREAT WRITERS ON THE ART OF FICTION: From Mark Twain to Joyce Carol Oates, Edited by James Daley. An indispensable source of advice and inspiration, this anthology features essays by Henry James, Kate Chopin, Willa Cather, Sinclair Lewis, Jack London, Raymond Chandler, Raymond Carver, Eudora Welty, and Kurt Vonnegut, Jr. 192pp. 5⅜ x 8½. 0-486-45128-3

HAMLET, William Shakespeare. The quintessential Shakespearean tragedy, whose highly charged confrontations and anguished soliloquies probe depths of human feeling rarely sounded in any art. Reprinted from an authoritative British edition complete with illuminating footnotes. 128pp. 5³⁄₁₆ x 8¼. 0-486-27278-8

THE HAUNTED HOUSE, Charles Dickens. A Yuletide gathering in an eerie country retreat provides the backdrop for Dickens and his friends — including Elizabeth Gaskell and Wilkie Collins — who take turns spinning supernatural yarns. 144pp. 5⅜ x 8½. 0-486-46309-5

Browse over 9,000 books at www.doverpublications.com

HEART OF DARKNESS, Joseph Conrad. Dark allegory of a journey up the Congo River and the narrator's encounter with the mysterious Mr. Kurtz. Masterly blend of adventure, character study, psychological penetration. For many, Conrad's finest, most enigmatic story. 80pp. 5¾₆ x 8¼. 0-486-26464-5

HENSON AT THE NORTH POLE, Matthew A. Henson. This thrilling memoir by the heroic African-American who was Peary's companion through two decades of Arctic exploration recounts a tale of danger, courage, and determination. "Fascinating and exciting." — *Commonweal.* 128pp. 5⅜ x 8½. 0-486-45472-X

HISTORIC COSTUMES AND HOW TO MAKE THEM, Mary Fernald and E. Shenton. Practical, informative guidebook shows how to create everything from short tunics worn by Saxon men in the fifth century to a lady's bustle dress of the late 1800s. 81 illustrations. 176pp. 5⅜ x 8½. 0-486-44906-8

THE HOUND OF THE BASKERVILLES, Arthur Conan Doyle. A deadly curse in the form of a legendary ferocious beast continues to claim its victims from the Baskerville family until Holmes and Watson intervene. Often called the best detective story ever written. 128pp. 5¾₆ x 8¼. 0-486-28214-7

THE HOUSE BEHIND THE CEDARS, Charles W. Chesnutt. Originally published in 1900, this groundbreaking novel by a distinguished African-American author recounts the drama of a brother and sister who "pass for white" during the dangerous days of Reconstruction. 208pp. 5⅜ x 8½. 0-486-46144-0

THE HUMAN FIGURE IN MOTION, Eadweard Muybridge. The 4,789 photographs in this definitive selection show the human figure — models almost all undraped — engaged in over 160 different types of action: running, climbing stairs, etc. 390pp. 7⅞ x 10⅝. 0-486-20204-6

THE IMPORTANCE OF BEING EARNEST, Oscar Wilde. Wilde's witty and buoyant comedy of manners, filled with some of literature's most famous epigrams, reprinted from an authoritative British edition. Considered Wilde's most perfect work. 64pp. 5¾₆ x 8¼. 0-486-26478-5

THE INFERNO, Dante Alighieri. Translated and with notes by Henry Wadsworth Longfellow. The first stop on Dante's famous journey from Hell to Purgatory to Paradise, this 14th-century allegorical poem blends vivid and shocking imagery with graceful lyricism. Translated by the beloved 19th-century poet, Henry Wadsworth Longfellow. 256pp. 5¾₆ x 8¼. 0-486-44288-8

JANE EYRE, Charlotte Brontë. Written in 1847, *Jane Eyre* tells the tale of an orphan girl's progress from the custody of cruel relatives to an oppressive boarding school and its culmination in a troubled career as a governess. 448pp. 5¾₆ x 8¼. 0-486-42449-9

JAPANESE WOODBLOCK FLOWER PRINTS, Tanigami Kônan. Extraordinary collection of Japanese woodblock prints by a well-known artist features 120 plates in brilliant color. Realistic images from a rare edition include daffodils, tulips, and other familiar and unusual flowers. 128pp. 11 x 8¼. 0-486-46442-3

JEWELRY MAKING AND DESIGN, Augustus F. Rose and Antonio Cirino. Professional secrets of jewelry making are revealed in a thorough, practical guide. Over 200 illustrations. 306pp. 5⅜ x 8½. 0-486-21750-7

JULIUS CAESAR, William Shakespeare. Great tragedy based on Plutarch's account of the lives of Brutus, Julius Caesar and Mark Antony. Evil plotting, ringing oratory, high tragedy with Shakespeare's incomparable insight, dramatic power. Explanatory footnotes. 96pp. 5¾₆ x 8¼. 0-486-26876-4

THE JUNGLE, Upton Sinclair. 1906 bestseller shockingly reveals intolerable labor practices and working conditions in the Chicago stockyards as it tells the grim story of a Slavic family that emigrates to America full of optimism but soon faces despair. 320pp. 5⁵⁄₁₆ x 8¼. 0-486-41923-1

THE KINGDOM OF GOD IS WITHIN YOU, Leo Tolstoy. The soul-searching book that inspired Gandhi to embrace the concept of passive resistance, Tolstoy's 1894 polemic clearly outlines a radical, well-reasoned revision of traditional Christian thinking. 352pp. 5⁵⁄₁₆ x 8¼. 0-486-45138-0

THE LADY OR THE TIGER?: and Other Logic Puzzles, Raymond M. Smullyan. Created by a renowned puzzle master, these whimsically themed challenges involve paradoxes about probability, time, and change; metapuzzles; and self-referentiality. Nineteen chapters advance in difficulty from relatively simple to highly complex. 1982 edition. 240pp. 5⅜ x 8½. 0-486-47027-X

LEAVES OF GRASS: The Original 1855 Edition, Walt Whitman. Whitman's immortal collection includes some of the greatest poems of modern times, including his masterpiece, "Song of Myself." Shattering standard conventions, it stands as an unabashed celebration of body and nature. 128pp. 5⁵⁄₁₆ x 8¼. 0-486-45676-5

LES MISÉRABLES, Victor Hugo. Translated by Charles E. Wilbour. Abridged by James K. Robinson. A convict's heroic struggle for justice and redemption plays out against a fiery backdrop of the Napoleonic wars. This edition features the excellent original translation and a sensitive abridgment. 304pp. 6⅛ x 9¼. 0-486-45789-3

LILITH: A Romance, George MacDonald. In this novel by the father of fantasy literature, a man travels through time to meet Adam and Eve and to explore humanity's fall from grace and ultimate redemption. 240pp. 5⅜ x 8½. 0-486-46818-6

THE LOST LANGUAGE OF SYMBOLISM, Harold Bayley. This remarkable book reveals the hidden meaning behind familiar images and words, from the origins of Santa Claus to the fleur-de-lys, drawing from mythology, folklore, religious texts, and fairy tales. 1,418 illustrations. 784pp. 5⅜ x 8½. 0-486-44787-1

MACBETH, William Shakespeare. A Scottish nobleman murders the king in order to succeed to the throne. Tortured by his conscience and fearful of discovery, he becomes tangled in a web of treachery and deceit that ultimately spells his doom. 96pp. 5⁵⁄₁₆ x 8¼. 0-486-27802-6

MAKING AUTHENTIC CRAFTSMAN FURNITURE: Instructions and Plans for 62 Projects, Gustav Stickley. Make authentic reproductions of handsome, functional, durable furniture: tables, chairs, wall cabinets, desks, a hall tree, and more. Construction plans with drawings, schematics, dimensions, and lumber specs reprinted from 1900s The Craftsman magazine. 128pp. 8⅛ x 11. 0-486-25000-8

MATHEMATICS FOR THE NONMATHEMATICIAN, Morris Kline. Erudite and entertaining overview follows development of mathematics from ancient Greeks to present. Topics include logic and mathematics, the fundamental concept, differential calculus, probability theory, much more. Exercises and problems. 641pp. 5⅜ x 8½. 0-486-24823-2

MEMOIRS OF AN ARABIAN PRINCESS FROM ZANZIBAR, Emily Ruete. This 19th-century autobiography offers a rare inside look at the society surrounding a sultan's palace. A real-life princess in exile recalls her vanished world of harems, slave trading, and court intrigues. 288pp. 5⅜ x 8½. 0-486-47121-7

Browse over 9,000 books at www.doverpublications.com

THE METAMORPHOSIS AND OTHER STORIES, Franz Kafka. Excellent new English translations of title story (considered by many critics Kafka's most perfect work), plus "The Judgment," "In the Penal Colony," "A Country Doctor," and "A Report to an Academy." Note. 96pp. 5⅛ x 8¼.   0-486-29030-1

MICROSCOPIC ART FORMS FROM THE PLANT WORLD, R. Anheisser. From undulating curves to complex geometrics, a world of fascinating images abound in this classic, illustrated survey of microscopic plants. Features 400 detailed illustrations of nature's minute but magnificent handiwork. The accompanying CD-ROM includes all of the images in the book. 128pp. 9 x 9.   0-486-46013-4

A MIDSUMMER NIGHT'S DREAM, William Shakespeare. Among the most popular of Shakespeare's comedies, this enchanting play humorously celebrates the vagaries of love as it focuses upon the intertwined romances of several pairs of lovers. Explanatory footnotes. 80pp. 5⅛ x 8¼.   0-486-27067-X

THE MONEY CHANGERS, Upton Sinclair. Originally published in 1908, this cautionary novel from the author of *The Jungle* explores corruption within the American system as a group of power brokers joins forces for personal gain, triggering a crash on Wall Street. 192pp. 5⅜ x 8½.   0-486-46917-4

THE MOST POPULAR HOMES OF THE TWENTIES, William A. Radford. With a New Introduction by Daniel D. Reiff. Based on a rare 1925 catalog, this architectural showcase features floor plans, construction details, and photos of 26 homes, plus articles on entrances, porches, garages, and more. 250 illustrations, 21 color plates. 176pp. 8⅜ x 11.   0-486-47028-8

MY 66 YEARS IN THE BIG LEAGUES, Connie Mack. With a New Introduction by Rich Westcott. A Founding Father of modern baseball, Mack holds the record for most wins — and losses — by a major league manager. Enhanced by 70 photographs, his warmhearted autobiography is populated by many legends of the game. 288pp. 5⅜ x 8½.   0-486-47184-5

NARRATIVE OF THE LIFE OF FREDERICK DOUGLASS, Frederick Douglass. Douglass's graphic depictions of slavery, harrowing escape to freedom, and life as a newspaper editor, eloquent orator, and impassioned abolitionist. 96pp. 5⅛ x 8¼.
                      0-486-28499-9

THE NIGHTLESS CITY: Geisha and Courtesan Life in Old Tokyo, J. E. de Becker. This unsurpassed study from 100 years ago ventured into Tokyo's red-light district to survey geisha and courtesan life and offer meticulous descriptions of training, dress, social hierarchy, and erotic practices. 49 black-and-white illustrations; 2 maps. 496pp. 5⅜ x 8½.   0-486-45563-7

THE ODYSSEY, Homer. Excellent prose translation of ancient epic recounts adventures of the homeward-bound Odysseus. Fantastic cast of gods, giants, cannibals, sirens, other supernatural creatures — true classic of Western literature. 256pp. 5⅛ x 8¼.
                      0-486-40654-7

OEDIPUS REX, Sophocles. Landmark of Western drama concerns the catastrophe that ensues when King Oedipus discovers he has inadvertently killed his father and married his mother. Masterly construction, dramatic irony. Explanatory footnotes. 64pp. 5⅛ x 8¼.   0-486-26877-2

ONCE UPON A TIME: The Way America Was, Eric Sloane. Nostalgic text and drawings brim with gentle philosophies and descriptions of how we used to live — self-sufficiently — on the land, in homes, and among the things built by hand. 44 line illustrations. 64pp. 8⅜ x 11.   0-486-44411-2

Browse over 9,000 books at www.doverpublications.com

ONE OF OURS, Willa Cather. The Pulitzer Prize–winning novel about a young Nebraskan looking for something to believe in. Alienated from his parents, rejected by his wife, he finds his destiny on the bloody battlefields of World War I. 352pp. 5³⁄₁₆ x 8¼. 0-486-45599-8

ORIGAMI YOU CAN USE: 27 Practical Projects, Rick Beech. Origami models can be more than decorative, and this unique volume shows how! The 27 practical projects include a CD case, frame, napkin ring, and dish. Easy instructions feature 400 two-color illustrations. 96pp. 8¼ x 11. 0-486-47057-1

OTHELLO, William Shakespeare. Towering tragedy tells the story of a Moorish general who earns the enmity of his ensign Iago when he passes him over for a promotion. Masterly portrait of an archvillain. Explanatory footnotes. 112pp. 5³⁄₁₆ x 8¼. 0-486-29097-2

PARADISE LOST, John Milton. Notes by John A. Himes. First published in 1667, *Paradise Lost* ranks among the greatest of English literature's epic poems. It's a sublime retelling of Adam and Eve's fall from grace and expulsion from Eden. Notes by John A. Himes. 480pp. 5³⁄₁₆ x 8¼. 0-486-44287-X

PASSING, Nella Larsen. Married to a successful physician and prominently ensconced in society, Irene Redfield leads a charmed existence — until a chance encounter with a childhood friend who has been "passing for white." 112pp. 5⅜ x 8½. 0-486-43713-2

PERSPECTIVE DRAWING FOR BEGINNERS, Len A. Doust. Doust carefully explains the roles of lines, boxes, and circles, and shows how visualizing shapes and forms can be used in accurate depictions of perspective. One of the most concise introductions available. 33 illustrations. 64pp. 5⅜ x 8½. 0-486-45149-6

PERSPECTIVE MADE EASY, Ernest R. Norling. Perspective is easy; yet, surprisingly few artists know the simple rules that make it so. Remedy that situation with this simple, step-by-step book, the first devoted entirely to the topic. 256 illustrations. 224pp. 5⅜ x 8½. 0-486-40473-0

THE PICTURE OF DORIAN GRAY, Oscar Wilde. Celebrated novel involves a handsome young Londoner who sinks into a life of depravity. His body retains perfect youth and vigor while his recent portrait reflects the ravages of his crime and sensuality. 176pp. 5³⁄₁₆ x 8¼. 0-486-27807-7

PRIDE AND PREJUDICE, Jane Austen. One of the most universally loved and admired English novels, an effervescent tale of rural romance transformed by Jane Austen's art into a witty, shrewdly observed satire of English country life. 272pp. 5³⁄₁₆ x 8¼. 0-486-28473-5

THE PRINCE, Niccolò Machiavelli. Classic, Renaissance-era guide to acquiring and maintaining political power. Today, nearly 500 years after it was written, this calculating prescription for autocratic rule continues to be much read and studied. 80pp. 5³⁄₁₆ x 8¼. 0-486-27274-5

QUICK SKETCHING, Carl Cheek. A perfect introduction to the technique of "quick sketching." Drawing upon an artist's immediate emotional responses, this is an extremely effective means of capturing the essential form and features of a subject. More than 100 black-and-white illustrations throughout. 48pp. 11 x 8¼. 0-486-46608-6

RANCH LIFE AND THE HUNTING TRAIL, Theodore Roosevelt. Illustrated by Frederic Remington. Beautifully illustrated by Remington, Roosevelt's celebration of the Old West recounts his adventures in the Dakota Badlands of the 1880s, from roundups to Indian encounters to hunting bighorn sheep. 208pp. 6¼ x 9¼. 0-486-47340-6

Browse over 9,000 books at www.doverpublications.com

THE RED BADGE OF COURAGE, Stephen Crane. Amid the nightmarish chaos of a Civil War battle, a young soldier discovers courage, humility, and, perhaps, wisdom. Uncanny re-creation of actual combat. Enduring landmark of American fiction. 112pp. 5³⁄₁₆ x 8¼. 0-486-26465-3

RELATIVITY SIMPLY EXPLAINED, Martin Gardner. One of the subject's clearest, most entertaining introductions offers lucid explanations of special and general theories of relativity, gravity, and spacetime, models of the universe, and more. 100 illustrations. 224pp. 5⅜ x 8½. 0-486-29315-7

REMBRANDT DRAWINGS: 116 Masterpieces in Original Color, Rembrandt van Rijn. This deluxe hardcover edition features drawings from throughout the Dutch master's prolific career. Informative captions accompany these beautifully reproduced landscapes, biblical vignettes, figure studies, animal sketches, and portraits. 128pp. 8⅜ x 11. 0-486-46149-1

THE ROAD NOT TAKEN AND OTHER POEMS, Robert Frost. A treasury of Frost's most expressive verse. In addition to the title poem: "An Old Man's Winter Night," "In the Home Stretch," "Meeting and Passing," "Putting in the Seed," many more. All complete and unabridged. 64pp. 5³⁄₁₆ x 8¼. 0-486-27550-7

ROMEO AND JULIET, William Shakespeare. Tragic tale of star-crossed lovers, feuding families and timeless passion contains some of Shakespeare's most beautiful and lyrical love poetry. Complete, unabridged text with explanatory footnotes. 96pp. 5³⁄₁₆ x 8¼. 0-486-27557-4

SANDITON AND THE WATSONS: Austen's Unfinished Novels, Jane Austen. Two tantalizing incomplete stories revisit Austen's customary milieu of courtship and venture into new territory, amid guests at a seaside resort. Both are worth reading for pleasure and study. 112pp. 5⅜ x 8½. 0-486-45793-1

THE SCARLET LETTER, Nathaniel Hawthorne. With stark power and emotional depth, Hawthorne's masterpiece explores sin, guilt, and redemption in a story of adultery in the early days of the Massachusetts Colony. 192pp. 5³⁄₁₆ x 8¼.
0-486-28048-9

THE SEASONS OF AMERICA PAST, Eric Sloane. Seventy-five illustrations depict cider mills and presses, sleds, pumps, stump-pulling equipment, plows, and other elements of America's rural heritage. A section of old recipes and household hints adds additional color. 160pp. 8⅜ x 11. 0-486-44220-9

SELECTED CANTERBURY TALES, Geoffrey Chaucer. Delightful collection includes the General Prologue plus three of the most popular tales: "The Knight's Tale," "The Miller's Prologue and Tale," and "The Wife of Bath's Prologue and Tale." In modern English. 144pp. 5³⁄₁₆ x 8¼. 0-486-28241-4

SELECTED POEMS, Emily Dickinson. Over 100 best-known, best-loved poems by one of America's foremost poets, reprinted from authoritative early editions. No comparable edition at this price. Index of first lines. 64pp. 5³⁄₁₆ x 8¼. 0-486-26466-1

SIDDHARTHA, Hermann Hesse. Classic novel that has inspired generations of seekers. Blending Eastern mysticism and psychoanalysis, Hesse presents a strikingly original view of man and culture and the arduous process of self-discovery, reconciliation, harmony, and peace. 112pp. 5³⁄₁₆ x 8¼. 0-486-40653-9

SKETCHING OUTDOORS, Leonard Richmond. This guide offers beginners step-by-step demonstrations of how to depict clouds, trees, buildings, and other outdoor sights. Explanations of a variety of techniques include shading and constructional drawing. 48pp. 11 x 8¼. 0-486-46922-0

Browse over 9,000 books at www.doverpublications.com

CATALOG OF DOVER BOOKS

SMALL HOUSES OF THE FORTIES: With Illustrations and Floor Plans, Harold E. Group. 56 floor plans and elevations of houses that originally cost less than $15,000 to build. Recommended by financial institutions of the era, they range from Colonials to Cape Cods. 144pp. 8⅜ x 11. 0-486-45598-X

SOME CHINESE GHOSTS, Lafcadio Hearn. Rooted in ancient Chinese legends, these richly atmospheric supernatural tales are recounted by an expert in Oriental lore. Their originality, power, and literary charm will captivate readers of all ages. 96pp. 5⅜ x 8½. 0-486-46306-0

SONGS FOR THE OPEN ROAD: Poems of Travel and Adventure, Edited by The American Poetry & Literacy Project. More than 80 poems by 50 American and British masters celebrate real and metaphorical journeys. Poems by Whitman, Byron, Millay, Sandburg, Langston Hughes, Emily Dickinson, Robert Frost, Shelley, Tennyson, Yeats, many others. Note. 80pp. 5³⁄₁₆ x 8¼. 0-486-40646-6

SPOON RIVER ANTHOLOGY, Edgar Lee Masters. An American poetry classic, in which former citizens of a mythical midwestern town speak touchingly from the grave of the thwarted hopes and dreams of their lives. 144pp. 5³⁄₁₆ x 8¼. 0-486-27275-3

STAR LORE: Myths, Legends, and Facts, William Tyler Olcott. Captivating retellings of the origins and histories of ancient star groups include Pegasus, Ursa Major, Pleiades, signs of the zodiac, and other constellations. "Classic." — Sky & Telescope. 58 illustrations. 544pp. 5⅜ x 8½. 0-486-43581-4

THE STRANGE CASE OF DR. JEKYLL AND MR. HYDE, Robert Louis Stevenson. This intriguing novel, both fantasy thriller and moral allegory, depicts the struggle of two opposing personalities — one essentially good, the other evil — for the soul of one man. 64pp. 5³⁄₁₆ x 8¼. 0-486-26688-5

SURVIVAL HANDBOOK: The Official U.S. Army Guide, Department of the Army. This special edition of the Army field manual is geared toward civilians. An essential companion for campers and all lovers of the outdoors, it constitutes the most authoritative wilderness guide. 288pp. 5³⁄₁₆ x 8¼. 0-486-46184-X

A TALE OF TWO CITIES, Charles Dickens. Against the backdrop of the French Revolution, Dickens unfolds his masterpiece of drama, adventure, and romance about a man falsely accused of treason. Excitement and derring-do in the shadow of the guillotine. 304pp. 5³⁄₁₆ x 8¼. 0-486-40651-2

TEN PLAYS, Anton Chekhov. *The Sea Gull, Uncle Vanya, The Three Sisters, The Cherry Orchard*, and *Ivanov*, plus 5 one-act comedies: *The Anniversary, An Unwilling Martyr, The Wedding, The Bear*, and *The Proposal*. 336pp. 5³⁄₁₆ x 8¼. 0-486-46560-8

THE FLYING INN, G. K. Chesterton. Hilarious romp in which pub owner Humphrey Hump and friend take to the road in a donkey cart filled with rum and cheese, inveighing against Prohibition and other "oppressive forms of modernity." 320pp. 5⅜ x 8½. 0-486-41910-X

THIRTY YEARS THAT SHOOK PHYSICS: The Story of Quantum Theory, George Gamow. Lucid, accessible introduction to the influential theory of energy and matter features careful explanations of Dirac's anti-particles, Bohr's model of the atom, and much more. Numerous drawings. 1966 edition. 240pp. 5⅜ x 8½. 0-486-24895-X

TREASURE ISLAND, Robert Louis Stevenson. Classic adventure story of a perilous sea journey, a mutiny led by the infamous Long John Silver, and a lethal scramble for buried treasure — seen through the eyes of cabin boy Jim Hawkins. 160pp. 5³⁄₁₆ x 8¼. 0-486-27559-0

Browse over 9,000 books at www.doverpublications.com

THE TRIAL, Franz Kafka. Translated by David Wyllie. From its gripping first sentence onward, this novel exemplifies the term "Kafkaesque." Its darkly humorous narrative recounts a bank clerk's entrapment in a bureaucratic maze, based on an undisclosed charge. 176pp. 5³⁄₁₆ x 8¼.   0-486-47061-X

THE TURN OF THE SCREW, Henry James. Gripping ghost story by great novelist depicts the sinister transformation of 2 innocent children into flagrant liars and hypocrites. An elegantly told tale of unspoken horror and psychological terror. 96pp. 5³⁄₁₆ x 8¼.   0-486-26684-2

UP FROM SLAVERY, Booker T. Washington. Washington (1856-1915) rose to become the most influential spokesman for African-Americans of his day. In this eloquently written book, he describes events in a remarkable life that began in bondage and culminated in worldwide recognition. 160pp. 5³⁄₁₆ x 8¼.   0-486-28738-6

VICTORIAN HOUSE DESIGNS IN AUTHENTIC FULL COLOR: 75 Plates from the "Scientific American – Architects and Builders Edition," 1885-1894, Edited by Blanche Cirker. Exquisitely detailed, exceptionally handsome designs for an enormous variety of attractive city dwellings, spacious suburban and country homes, charming "cottages" and other structures — all accompanied by perspective views and floor plans. 80pp. 9¼ x 12¼.   0-486-29438-2

VILLETTE, Charlotte Brontë. Acclaimed by Virginia Woolf as "Brontë's finest novel," this moving psychological study features a remarkably modern heroine who abandons her native England for a new life as a schoolteacher in Belgium. 480pp. 5³⁄₁₆ x 8¼.   0-486-45557-2

THE VOYAGE OUT, Virginia Woolf. A moving depiction of the thrills and confusion of youth, Woolf's acclaimed first novel traces a shipboard journey to South America for a captivating exploration of a woman's growing self-awareness. 288pp. 5³⁄₁₆ x 8¼.   0-486-45005-8

WALDEN; OR, LIFE IN THE WOODS, Henry David Thoreau. Accounts of Thoreau's daily life on the shores of Walden Pond outside Concord, Massachusetts, are interwoven with musings on the virtues of self-reliance and individual freedom, on society, government, and other topics. 224pp. 5³⁄₁₆ x 8¼.   0-486-28495-6

WILD PILGRIMAGE: A Novel in Woodcuts, Lynd Ward. Through startling engravings shaded in black and red, Ward wordlessly tells the story of a man trapped in an industrial world, struggling between the grim reality around him and the fantasies his imagination creates. 112pp. 6⅛ x 9¼.   0-486-46583-7

WILLY POGÁNY REDISCOVERED, Willy Pogány. Selected and Edited by Jeff A. Menges. More than 100 color and black-and-white Art Nouveau–style illustrations from fairy tales and adventure stories include scenes from Wagner's "Ring" cycle, *The Rime of the Ancient Mariner, Gulliver's Travels,* and *Faust.* 144pp. 8⅜ x 11.
                                                           0-486-47046-6

WOOLLY THOUGHTS: Unlock Your Creative Genius with Modular Knitting, Pat Ashforth and Steve Plummer. Here's the revolutionary way to knit — easy, fun, and foolproof! Beginners and experienced knitters need only master a single stitch to create their own designs with patchwork squares. More than 100 illustrations. 128pp. 6½ x 9¼.   0-486-46084-3

WUTHERING HEIGHTS, Emily Brontë. Somber tale of consuming passions and vengeance — played out amid the lonely English moors — recounts the turbulent and tempestuous love story of Cathy and Heathcliff. Poignant and compelling. 256pp. 5³⁄₁₆ x 8¼.   0-486-29256-8